THE DANC
OF KIOWA

"Marshal, yo

The voice c

"Be sensible, Marshal. We got nothin' against you; all we want's the prisoner."

That was another voice, smoother, more experienced than the first, and it came from the left. Cross-fire. The pattern was as obvious as it was deadly.

Kiowa was sweating again. And Bobby Jack Wilkes was grinning. Kiowa loaded the short-barrelled .44-40, then dug some of the clay and grass out of the revolver and hoped that it would fire at least a few times before exploding.

CLIFTON ADAMS

The Dangerous Days of Kiowa Jones

FONTANA / Collins

First published in Great Britain 1964
First issued in Fontana Books 1966
Second Impression September 1973

Printed in Great Britain
Collins Clear-Type Press London and Glasgow

Let it be duly noted that all characters directly implicated in the action of this novel were invented by the author. This holds true, of course, in the case of Rupe Dobie, the fictional hangman. It is not intended that Dobie should resemble any real person, living or dead, including the talented Mr. George Maledon, that hardy little Bavarian who laboured so long and conscientiously at Fort Smith's renowned hanging machine.

C.A.

CHAPTER ONE

IN THE SUMMER of his eighteenth year Bobby Jack Wilkes made an important discovery. He had a talent for killing.

He soon developed a deadly touch with weapons. He had a certain feeling for guns, a flair for ropes, a genius with knives. Not surprisingly, Bobby Jack rose quickly to the top of his chosen profession. He was an assassin.

By the time he was nineteen Wilkes had killed twelve human beings: men, women and children. It was said that he was the highest-paid assassin on the Great Plains during the early '80s—and this could be believed. His name was known in great ranch houses from the Dakotas to the Gulf, in cattlemen's associations, in board rooms and presidential suites of certain railroad and express companies. Wherever powerful men had enemies, wherever competition became too insistent, wherever strong wills clashed, in those places the name of Bobby Jack Wilkes would be well known.

It might be said that the early years—the time between his eighteenth and twenty-first birthdays—were Bobby Jack's Golden Years. Then, for reasons difficult to explain, the young assassin's fortunes began to sour.

A county sheriff down in Laredo, riled over the murder of a friend, had shown surprising grit, and Bobby Jack had been forced to beat an undignified retreat. Then, up on the Trinity, a killing had gone wrong—a case of mistaken identity—and it had been necessary to return and do the job over. Always a dangerous business. Finally there had been an unhappy affair with the Mex sheepmen up in the Panhandle. And a bounty hunter killed in Tascosa, an unfortunate and unprofitable business that forced Bobby Jack once more to ride the ridges. But the cruellest turn of all was when he had come down with Indian fever over on the Comanche-Apache reservation below Fort Sill, and got himself captured by a deputy U.S.

Marshal who was riding for a federal court almost four hundred miles away.

So it wasn't much wonder that the young killer's disposition had taken a wolfish turn. For twelve days he'd been travelling shank's mare, eating the dust of the marshal's horse and two pack animals, handcuffed and leg-ironed, and chained to two other prisoners that the lawman had picked up along the way. Heading for old Izaac Parker's court in Fort Smith—the toughest court, the toughest judge on the frontier, with a record for hanging second to none in the United States.

Behind Bobby Jack, their leg chains linking them together, stumbled a wizened, mournful little hunky with the once honourable name of Levi Skodaschinski, but now no longer honourable and long since shortened to just Skoda. Levi Skoda was—or had been—a gambler. Now he was a murderer. He had killed his wife, a beautiful, fiery gipsy outcast, and now Levi himself was about to die. This one thing he knew. Before the moon came full two times, he would be dead. The tarot had told him so.

Behind Skoda, and last in the grim procession, limped a fat, wheezing nobody called Milo Preston. Milo was an unlicensed trader who had been running whisky to the Plains Cheyennes, and to the Quahada Comanches who still hadn't completely given up the notion of breaking loose of the reservation.

They were a weary, bedraggled lot by the time they had crossed the Big Pasture country and stopped on the Washita for a day's rest. This wasn't the way the marshal had planned it, making the prisoners tramp clear across the Indian Nations, not to mention a big piece of Comanche reservation, all the way to Fort Smith. To start with there had been a wagon, but the team had spooked and broken a wheel and an axle, and there had been no place closer than Fort Cill to get it fixed. Chote Duncan, the U.S. Marshal, had decided to set the prisoners afoot and try to rent or borrow another wagon at Stonewall, a way station on the old stage road that linked with the Katy Railroad in the Choctaw Nation.

But this had been a jinxed trip from the beginning, although it hadn't seemed so at first. Relatives of Bobby Jack's murder victims had put a thousand-dollar bounty on the assassin's head. To Chote Duncan, a man who seldom earned more than thirty dollars a month, landing the famous killer had seemed a dazzling stroke of good fortune.

Now he wasn't so sure. All day a big sickness had been growing in his gut. His head pounded, his mouth was dry, he had trouble getting his eyes to focus properly. The young assassin watched him closely. Every time Chote Duncan looked back to check on the prisoners, Bobby Jack's china-blue eyes would be fixed on the marshal's face. Toward mid-afternoon the killer began to smile.

"You ain't lookin' so good, Marshal. You ain't ailin', are you?"

Marshal Duncan, a blunt, thick-featured man in his early forties, pulled himself erect in the saddle. "Don't get your hopes up, Wilkes. A gut ache's not goin' to save you from old Izaac Parker's hangin' machine."

Bobby Jack Wilkes said nothing but kept smiling. And the next morning the marshal allowed they'd lay over on the Washita and take a day's rest.

"You think a day's rest'll fix you up, Marshal?"

Duncan lay back against his saddle, watching his prisoners, a shotgun across his lap. He knew now that he had caught the fever that had felled Wilkes. Indian fever, Bobby Jack had called it. Smallpox. Duncan hadn't believed him. The sickness had left no pocks on the killer's body.

"Indian fever's a funny thing," Bobby Jack told him. "A light case can wear itself out without leavin' its mark. You've got it, Duncan." He smiled again, carefully calculating the disease's progress.

Milo Preston, with bugged eyes, stared at Bobby Jack and the marshal. "Marshal, you got to turn us loose! You can't leave us here to die without givin' us a chance, just because you went and caught smallpox!"

The marshal said coldly, "Shut up, Preston. If I've got smallpox, all right, I've got it. But I'll live through it; don't worry yourself about that. And I'll get you all back safe and sound to Fort Smith. Don't worry yourself about that, either."

Bobby Jack laughed softly. The plague had touched him lightly, left him immune. He had nothing to fear.

For Levi Skoda it was a matter of no importance. The question of his death had already been settled, in the tarot.

Duncan kept his prisoners in leg irons and chained them to a salt-cedar trunk on the south bank of the Washita. The muscles of the marshal's arms knotted and began to jump, and soon the cramping had spread to all parts of his body. This was the way it started—first the rigors, then the vomiting and fever. Smallpox. There was no doubt about it now.

Deaf to Preston's hysterical blubbering, blind to the assassin's steely smile of victory, the marshal got himself to his feet and made himself keep going until everything possible had been done. He had seen enough of smallpox to know what to expect. He stripped his horse and pack animals and set them free. Time enough to worry about being set afoot when and if he managed to live through the next ten to twelve days. Food and water were put within reach of the prisoners. Duncan threw his own roll and set out water and food for himself.

"What if you die?" Milo Preston demanded. "What's goin' to happen to us?"

It was Duncan's turn to smile, if weakly. He was in no frame of mind to fret over two murderers and a smuggler. He had problems of his own, and he could expect no help from anyone. Even if some stray rider chanced to pass this way, he'd wheel and run the minute he smelled the plague.

A black sickness boiled up inside him. After the vomiting came the fever, and the splitting head, and the fluttering pulse, and the great aching pain in the loins and back. There would be three or four days of this, if he lived that long, and then the characteristic running sores would begin to appear.

: : : :

It was on the fourth day that Kiowa Jones, with forty-five hard-earned dollars in his pocket and at peace with the world, sighted the three horses grazing along the Washita bottom. Taking a ranch hand's normal interest in loose stock, he reined toward the river to get a better look at the brands.

Government animals, two of them, with most of the hair rubbed off the topside. Pack animals. The third horse wore a Rafter-C on its hip. Maybe an Army officer from Sill out on a scouting expedition of some kind. Long way from home to be set afoot—if that was the case.

Kiowa paused and thoughtfully scratched the stubble on his jutting chin. He shrugged. Might as well have a look-see. He wasn't going anywhere anyway, except maybe up to Caldwell where he'd throw his money away on three-card monte and bar whisky and maybe a mess of fried chicken . . . if some dance-hall girl didn't get to him first.

Kiowa Jones, just easing over to the shady side of thirty, a man with not much of a past and even less of a future. Likeable kind of bird, so the general opinion went, but short on get-up-and-go. A fair example of a breed that was already becoming scarce in the changing cow country—the itinerant ranch hand. Loyal enough when on a job, but wearing no man's brand. Reasonably honest, hard enough worker, a good hand with livestock. But fiddle-footed. A drifter.

That was Kiowa Jones. The past few months he'd been riding windmills over in the Panhandle; then one day he took to thinking about the Indian Nations, so he drew his time and rode. And here he was, travelling with pleasant aimlessness along the Washita bottom, and it was spring and the land was green, and he was thinking what a fine notion it had been to get away from the pressures of steady work.

About that time he saw the horses. And a queer thing happened. For an instant he almost wished that he was back riding windmills.

But the feeling passed and Kiowa eased his big roan back along the meandering trail left by the grazing horses. He came upon the party suddenly—rounded a tangle of possum grapevines and wild-plum saplings, and there they were, three of them chained hand-to-hand around a salt cedar, the fourth off a piece in the brush.

The figure in the brush didn't move. Kiowa studied the chained men with slitted eyes. The fat, greedy-eyed Preston, now burning with fever and almost paralyzed with fear. The fatalistic Levi Skoda, in his own mind already dead, but to all appearances sound and healthy. Kiowa grunted involuntarily with indignation when his inspection reached the third of the chained trio.

"Mister . . . help us!"

It was a boyish voice, a boyish face, with only a downy hint of beard. What kind of a set-to is this, Kiowa asked angrily to himself. What kind of man would chain a helpless boy like that to a murderous-looking hunky and a man who was obviously down with a bad sickness?

"Mister . . .!" the boy called again. The hunky didn't even bother to look up. The fat man worked his mouth frantically but could only babble.

Kiowa's first impulse was to go immediately to the boy and get him loose from the others, but a long habit of minding his own business caused him to hesitate. He kneed in a little closer and noted the leg irons. Prisoners. Probably the body in the brush was a government marshal. Some of Kiowa's indignation began to cool.

"Mister!" the boy kept calling. "Mister, help us!"

But this time Kiowa reined toward the brush. Now he caught the stench of the disease, and so did the roan. The big gelding shied, lowered his head and tried to hunch his back. The rider reined him down with no nonsense.

Smallpox. The smell was unmistakable, and never pleasant, but for Kiowa it held no particular fear. He had been exposed to it before and apparently he was one of the lucky few who were immune. Still, around smallpox, it was never a mistake to use caution.

Kiowa got down and tied the roan to a whiplike sapling. "He's dead!" the young prisoner was calling anxiously. "Mister, there ain't anythin' you can do for him!"

But when Kiowa came closer he saw that the eyes, at least, were alive. The sores had appeared on the marshal's forehead and along the hairline. For the moment the fever had broken, but in another day or so the sores would become flowing, stinking pustules that would spread over his face and body. And the fever would come again, hotter than ever, and that was when the matter of living or dying would be decided.

The faded eyes looked up at the tall, gangling stranger. The mouth worked several times before he managed: "Smallpox, mister. I could do with some water, if you're a-mind, but don't come too close."

A water bucket near the marshal's roll had been overturned, probably during the first day of delirium. Kiowa took it up, filled it at the river and brought it back. "Spring rain's got the river up to half bank." He dipped water into a tin cup and handed it to the lawman. "A little muddy, but wet, I guess."

The marshal wouldn't reach for the cup until Kiowa said, "I've been around Indian fever before. Looks like it won't have me."

The marshal looked doubtful but drank and lay back in exhaustion. "Who are you?"

"Name of Jones. Kiowa—name, not tribe. Been ridin' the mills over in the Panhandle, till I took a notion to see some country. When did the fever break?"

"This mornin'." It was barely a whisper. "Jones, I'm done for. I won't last half a day when the fever starts again. You got to do somethin' for me."

Looking vaguely uncomfortable, Kiowa hunkered down and began building a brown-paper cigarette. "I ain't no lawdog, Marshal. I ride a little fence, grease the mills, nurse the cows and maybe now and then peel a bronc. But I ain't no lawdog."

"Jones, you got to get my prisoners to Fort Smith."

Kiowa felt in his hatband for a match. "That kind of brings up a question of my own. What kind of prisoners are they? I mean, what've they done that they have to be chained up the way they are?"

The marshal studied him wearily, without comprehension. "What kind are they? Two murderers. The other's a whisky runner."

Kiowa's indignation returned, this time laced with anger. "Murderers! That boy, what'd he do—bring in a few jars of white mule to liven up a country dance? Is that anything to chain him to two murderers for, and one of them startin' to come down with smallpox hisself?"

Marshal Chote Duncan fixed the lanky cowhand with a blank stare, the kind of look that professional men like to use on laymen who try to tell them their business. "That boy," he said in a steely whisper, "has got maybe twenty killin's to his credit, and don't ever show him your back, Jones, or you'll be twenty-one." He allowed himself a flinty smile. "That *boy*. There's a thousand-dollar bounty on him for the man that can get him to Smith in shape to hang. Bobby Jack Wilkes. That name mean somethin' to you, Jones?"

Kiowa blinked. That smooth-faced, helpless-looking boy—Bobby Jack Wilkes?

"A thousand dollars," the marshal breathed. "Yours, Jones. If you get him to Fort Smith."

Money figures that went above the price of an honest saddle held little meaning for Kiowa. The prospect of sudden riches failed to move him. The money would last only until he hit the nearest honky-tonk or crooked faro layout—he knew himself well enough for that.

"How about it?" Chote Duncan asked wearily. "A thousand dollars." He closed his eyes, thinking of the things he himself had planned to do with that money. A piece of cotton land up on the Neosho. The pleasant prospect of one peaceful day following another, and never worrying whether the next bullet would be the one with his name on it. And a certain girl just across the Missouri line . . .

He looked again at the homely cowhand. "How about it, Jones?"

"I was thinkin' about the fat man you got chained to the others. Which one's he?"

"Milo Preston, the smuggler. You sure it's the fever he's got?"

Kiowa shook his head. "We'll know sometime to-morrow. You mind if I stake him out from the others a-piece?"

The marshal managed an exhausted shrug. "Key's in my saddlebag. So're the circulars and arrest warrants, in case you've got any doubts about that pretty-faced killer."

Kiowa ploughed self-consciously through Duncan's personal plunder. Razor, soap, a change of socks, a moderately clean shirt. At the bottom of the bag were a dozen or more warrants issued by the Arkansas court and five "wanted" circulars, one of which concerned itself with Robert John (Bobby Jack) Wilkes. Age twenty-two, weight one hundred fifty, height five feet nine inches. Light hair, fair complexion, blue eyes. (But the eyes weren't blue, as Kiowa discovered later. Sometimes they were grey and sometimes green, and sometimes they seemed only to reflect whatever colour they were looking at. Strange eyes. What old-timers called cat eyes.) Wanted by sheriffs' offices in Texas, Kansas and Nebraska, among other places, and by the federal court in Fort Smith—for murder.

It was hard to believe. But there it was in black and white, and Kiowa Jones, like most men of meagre education, set great store in the printed word. He sighed and replaced all the plunder but the key.

The marshal didn't move or make a sound as Kiowa tramped upstream to where the prisoners were chained. Bobby Jack Wilkes turned an angelic face to the lanky cowhand and spoke huskily with the voice of a choirboy. "Thank the Lord, mister! You've come to help us after all, ain't you?"

Even now, after seeing the circulars and warrants, Kiowa was tempted to discount the marshal's warning as the babbling of a dying man—until his gaze met straight-on with that of Wilkes, and Kiowa saw a killer wolf watching him through the eyes of a boy. It was a shock, like suddenly coming on a big mountain cat on a dark path. Seeing the look on Kiowa's face, Bobby Jack threw back his head and laughed—a startling, musical, schoolboyish sound—straight up from the pit.

"What's the matter, cowboy? You look like you just swallowed a worm."

The fat man, Preston, babbled, "I want loose from here! There's a mistake somewhere. I'm not supposed to be here." His face was flushed, his eyes had that vague, glassy look that went with a soaring fever.

Kiowa side-stepped the young assassin as he might slip past a sleeping copperhead. Quickly, he unlocked Preston's leg iron and handcuffs, led the fat man about a hundred yards upstream and bedded him down. "God bless you!" the smuggler blubbered. "I'll not forget this, sir. You'll be rewarded. Well rewarded . . ."

"Sure, sure," Kiowa said sourly. He clapped the leg iron on again, but Preston didn't appear to notice. He went on with his mumbling, apparently believing that he was a free man.

Bobby Jack beamed a saintly smile as Kiowa headed back in their direction. "How about loosening our cuffs, cowboy? You wouldn't want us to die of gangrene and miss a good hangin', would you?"

The boy held out his hands. They were blue, cold and lifeless from lack of circulation. Grudgingly, Kiowa knelt and let the cuffs out a notch. He looked at the other prisoner. "How about you, mister? Let's see your hands."

Obediently, the melancholy hunky held out his hands and Kiowa loosened the cuffs. "What about the marshal?" Bobby Jack asked pleasantly. "How much longer, you figure, before he cashes in?"

"What makes you think he's goin' to die?"

The young killer shrugged, rubbing his tingling hands as the blood began to flow. "I can tell." He grinned disarmingly. "If you don't believe me, ask old Levi there. He knows everything."

The hunky looked at Kiowa, his eyes coming slowly into focus. At last he spoke, in an accent thick and guttural and strange to Kiowa's ears. "Levi Skoda. Once it was Skodaschinski, a long time ago."

Kiowa scratched his chin, studying the hunky, sensing the quiet, gentle man behind the angry shell. "You really know everything, like your friend says?"

"Call me murderer," Levi Skoda said softly, "but I am no assassin. And no friend of assassins. Still . . ." He shrugged, glancing at Bobby Jack's beaming face. "He's right. The marshal will die. The fever came on him on the fourth day of the new moon. He never had a chance." He spoke as though the marshal's death were already a fact.

"What's the fourth day of the new moon got to do with it?"

Bobby Jack laughed. "Old Levi here's a witchman, cowboy. A regular hoodoo, like that gipsy wife of his—the one he killed. Ain't that right, Levi?"

Skoda's expression didn't change, but Kiowa felt something go hard and cold inside the little hunky. "The marshal keeps my tarot in his war bag. Any reason why I can't use it while we're waitin' here?"

Kiowa squinted at the strange word.

Skoda smiled sadly. "Tarot. Or *tarocco*. Fortune-telling cards."

Bobby Jack grinned. "What did I tell you? A goddam witchman."

CHAPTER TWO

U.S. DEPUTY CHOTE DUNCAN lay motionless, his gaze fixed on the brilliant blue sky. A great golden eagle, straying over from its home grounds in the Ouachitas, cut a long graceful arc in space, watching for rabbits or ground squirrels or other small game. Waiting for something to move . . . or to die. Well, Duncan thought to himself, anyhow an eagle was better than a buzzard.

"How you feelin', Marshal?"

With great effort, Duncan adjusted the focus of his eyes. "The prisoners all right, Jones?"

Kiowa had to get down on one knee, the voice was so weak. "Fine. All but Preston. He looks more like a case of smallpox all the time."

It was the marshal's private opinion that Kiowa Jones was a damn' fool and maybe weak in the head to boot for playing so loose and easy with a disease like smallpox. But fool or not, Duncan was grateful for whatever help he could get. "You been thinkin' it over, Jones? About takin' the prisoners to Fort Smith?"

"It's not my line of work, Marshal. I'll stick around, though, and kind of look after things till you're ready to ride again."

Duncan closed his eyes. "I told you, Jones, my string's played out. If I die—when I die—what do you aim to do then?"

Kiowa pushed back his battered hat and rubbed his face. "Well, it's not so far to Stonewall. I could see the prisoners that far, and the stage could take a message to Fort Smith."

Wearily, the marshal shook his head. "You show up in a place like Stonewall and bounty hunters'll shoot Wilkes right out of your hands. Or maybe the other way around." The look that he fixed on Kiowa's face was long and thoughtful. "I've got no choice," he said at last. "I'll have to trust you, Jones. That thousand-dollar scalp money on Wilkes ain't half your worry."

Kiowa scowled. "It ain't?"

"Months ago, maybe years ago, Wilkes looked ahead to a time just like this, and prepared for it. Even a man like Bobby Jack Wilkes takes a wrong turn once in a while, makes a mistake that might get him caught by the law. And Wilkes knew it. So he started passin' the word around that, if such a day ever came, he'd pay double bounty to the man that busted him loose."

Kiowa whistled softly. "Two thousand dollars! How'd a prisoner figure to raise that kind of money?"

A fleeting, bitter smile touched the marshal's lips. "He packed it with him. In gold. A hundred double eagles. Word of that got passed around, too."

"Did he have it when you caught him?"

Duncan nodded. "I've got it buried in the bottom of my grain sack. You beginnin' to see how the scheme works? You see the nail it hangs us on?"

The picture was taking ugly, deadly shape in Kiowa's mind. If Duncan got back to Fort Smith without the gold, they'd figure he'd stolen it. If he got back without Wilkes *or* the gold, they'd figure the marshal had killed Wilkes and pocketed the money. Unless Wilkes was to show up later, alive, which would prove that the marshal had sold the killer his freedom. To come out of this thing with his whole hide, Duncan would have to show up at Smith with Wilkes *and* the gold. A tall order.

Kiowa shuffled uncomfortably. It looked like Duncan's good name was about all he had—and he wouldn't have that long, if somebody didn't get back to Smith with the true story. *And* Bobby Jack Wilkes. *And* the gold.

His eyes closed, the marshal said, "I need your help, Jones. I'm askin' for it."

It was a statement, not a question. It didn't require an immediate decision.

: : : :

Kiowa peeled the roan and staked the animal in the lush buffalo grass along the river. There was still plenty of game in the Nations and it was no problem to bag a brace of squirrels and a sage hen, even with his out-of-line and slightly rusty saddle rifle. Back at camp he built up a fire of driftwood and started a broth to simmering in the marshal's cooking pot. All Kiowa carried with him in the way of utensils was a small skillet, which he would use later for hoecake bread.

"By the way," he asked the marshal, "is it all right to let Skoda have his hoodoo cards?"

Duncan made a small sound and nodded. Then he held out a silver dollar and dropped it into Kiowa's surprised hand.

"What's this for?"

"U.S. Marshals are authorized to hire possemen. Out of their own pockets, of course, and that dollar happens to be all I've got with me. I offered it to you, and you accepted it." He handed Kiowa a small piece of paper, a label from a tobacco sack with some scribbling and a signature on the back. "Here it is in writing, Jones."

Kiowa scowled at the tobacco label, holding it at arm's length, as though it were a live cottonmouth at shedding time. "What is it?"

"Proof, if you ever need it, that you're my posseman, acting on my orders. When I die—if I die—that paper, for most practical purposes, makes you a United States Deputy Marshal."

"Now look here!" Kiowa started indignantly. But the marshal wasn't listening. He had closed his eyes and was unconscious, or sleeping, or playing possum. . . . Kiowa eyed the paper with dark suspicion. He must have been loco to stop here in the first place. A smallpox camp, a dying lawman, a woman-killer and a professional assassin. Kiowa Jones, after spending the best part of a lifetime maintaining his independence and avoiding responsibilities, sporting a U.S. Marshal's badge on his vest front. He could already hear the boys back in the Tascosa saloons, laughing fit to bust a cinch buckle.

: : : :

It was a long, long night there on the spring-green banks of the Washita. Kiowa had done all he could for Duncan and Preston, and now he hunkered near a driftwood fire with the prisoners, sipping scalding coffee from granite cups. Bobby Jack lay back in his chains, gazing blankly at the star-scattered sky. Occasionally he would grin at Kiowa, those queer eyes probing, testing the cowhand's steel.

Levi Skoda concentrated on his cards—those cards, well worn and brightly coloured, much like the ordinary cards used in poker and other gambling games, and at the same time not like them at all. With these cards Levi Skodaschinski had a certain knowing touch, a talent, just as sure and unexplainable as Bobby Jack's talent with weapons. His mother, in her Bohemian gipsy way, had sensed it on the day of his birth, and she had called him after the first master of the tarot, Eliphas Levi.

Skoda laid the cards out in the old way, the ancient way, with a ritual that was already old when the first Egyptian dynasty had been robust and young. The King of Pentacles, Money, representing a mature man neither dark nor light, but less light than dark—in this case representing Marshal Chote Duncan. In an elaborate fan-shaped pattern the cards began to fall, a life flowing through the little hunky's slender fingers.

Kiowa Jones watched with a puzzled frown as the pattern took shape on the horse blanket that Skoda used for a table. Odd cards with queer pictures on them. Some of the pictures Kiowa was able to puzzle out with little effort—the moon, the star, the tower, the hanging man. But the hanging man was hanging upside-down, and the tower was being struck by lightning, and other pictures appeared unfinished or too poorly drawn to make out. Kiowa grinned fleetingly to himself, envisioning the ruckus such a deck would raise in a Tascosa gambling house.

From the very beginning there were more swords than anything else in the pattern. Swords for violence, trouble, sometimes death. They fell in small clusters, punctuated with a scattering of Sceptres and Cups, but not many Pentacles. Except near the end. The cards marked with bright gold coins fell in a cluster of their own. Levi Skoda frowned. Was it possible that Duncan could overcome the curse of the fourth day and live to collect the bounty on Bobby Jack Wilkes, as the cards now indicated? Slowly, thoughtfully, Levi let the next card fall. It came down like a hammer, unexpected, the most disastrous card in the tarot. The lightning-struck tower.

Levi breathed deeply. Now the tarot's meaning was clear. *La Torre,* disaster, had fallen before the promise of riches could be developed. Levi was certain that the next card would be *La Morte,* death, but he didn't want to see it. He scooped the cards in nimble fingers, blocked them and began a careful, patient shuffling.

Bobby Jack raised himself to one elbow and grinned at Skoda. "Tell me somethin', Skoda. You really put any stock in all that hoodoo?"

Levi shrugged. "It's an ancient art, dealin' the tarot. There's folks that say you can see whatever you want to see in the cards, and maybe that's so—for some. But for me the cards don't lie. I've got the gift."

"The gift." Bobby Jack grinned sarcastically. "You're just a dumb hunky, Levi. Where you get off settin' yourself above others?"

Skoda shrugged again and smiled, but it was a mask smiling.

"What do the cards say about me?" the assassin asked dryly.

Levi spread his hands, the mask smiling. "*La Morte.*"

"Don't talk spick to me, hunky."

Now Skoda's voice took on a smooth, cool edge. "Italian. The best cards are Italian, not Spanish. It means death."

Bobby Jack shot a quick sidelong glance at Skoda but

didn't drop his sarcastic grin. "What do the cards say about the marshal?"

"*La Morte.*" In the same cool tone.

"And what do they say about *you,* hunky?"

Levi Skoda sighed. "*La Morte.*"

Bobby Jack lifted his head, wolflike, and howled with laughter. "Some goddamn packa cards you got there, Levi. *La Morte, La Morte, La Morte!* What about the cowhand? Is he *La Morte* too?"

Kiowa Jones, until that moment only mildly interested in the exchange, began to take closer notice.

But Skoda only shook his head. "I don't ask the tarot about people I like."

Bobby Jack laughed again. Kiowa breathed a bit easier—not that he put any stock in hoodoo, of course. He stood up, stretched, then tramped upstream to have a last look at Preston before turning in.

The fat man was in a bad way, thrashing about on the grass pallet that Kiowa had made for him, burning with fever. "Preston, anything I can do for you before turnin' in?"

Frightened blubbering was all the smuggler could manage. "Help me, help me!" He tried to sit up but Kiowa pushed him down.

"Take it easy, mister. The worst'll be over by mornin'." Kiowa soaked a piece of tarp from the marshal's pack rig and put it on the smuggler's face. There was nothing more to be done for Preston, so he headed back downstream to have a look at the marshal.

"Duncan, I'm about to turn in. Anything you want?"

The marshal said nothing.

"Duncan . . .?"

The marshal was silent.

After a while Kiowa headed back to the salt cedar to put the cuffs back on the prisoners and make sure they wouldn't be wandering about in the night.

Bobby Jack, with usual cynicism, said, "How're your patients doin', cowboy?"

"The fever's hit Preston. He's got hard times ahead."

"How about the marshal?"

Kiowa sighed and spread his hands, as Levi Skoda had done a few minutes before. "*La Morte,*" he said.

: : : :

There wasn't much sense in trying to sleep. Preston, tossing about in the brush, half out of his head with fever and crazy with fear, kept them all awake. Bobby Jack complained profanely. Levi Skoda gazed fixedly into the dying campfire, keeping his strange and foreign thoughts to himself.

"Dammit, Jones," Bobby Jack yelled, "why don't you put that fat bastard out of his misery so we can get some rest!"

Wearily, Kiowa stamped into his boots and built up the fire. "Killin' people," he said pointedly, glaring at the young assassin, "don't happen to be my line of work."

Suddenly Bobby Jack grinned. "I'd be glad to oblige, cowboy. If you'd just kind of unlock these leg irons . . ."

Kiowa turned away and spat, ridding himself of the taste of disgust. Then, half-asleep, he blundered along the river-bank to where he had bedded Preston down.

"Help me!" the smuggler blubbered. "Don't let me die!"

Kiowa wet the tarp again and put it on the fat man's forehead. "Take it easy. You got a good chance of beatin' the fever, if you don't go and scare yourself to death."

But fear had dug its talons in the smuggler's guts and wouldn't be shaken. "Listen to me, Jones! I've got money. I'll pay you. But don't let me die!"

Kiowa went through the marshal's things again, looking for medicine, but all he found was some axle-grease salve for horse-doctoring. Shortly before sunup Preston's fever reached its peak. Suddenly he yelled like a Comanche and tried to get to his feet, but Kiowa held him down.

"Jones, help me, I'm dyin'!"

"Mister, you haven't even started to get sick yet," Kiowa told him. "Give yourself another week, then you can talk about dyin'." Kiowa walked off a few paces, built and lit a cigarette. Nothing could be done until the fever broke, and maybe not then. Several minutes slipped away in the darkness. Gradually, Preston was quieting down—maybe slipping into unconsciousness. Kiowa had seen them lie like the dead for hours, even days, before the change came. He built another cigarette, smoked it quickly and returned to the smuggler.

"Preston, you all right?"

A shaft of moonlight filtered through the glittering leaves of a live oak and fell on the smuggler's face. It was as pale as calf tallow.

"Preston?"

Kiowa knelt and felt the fat man's forehead. It was already cool and clammy, and dead as stone. Slowly, Kiowa got to his feet. "Another grave to dig," he said quietly to himself, but not without feeling. On the reservations he had seen death enough from disease, and sometimes violence. As a cowhand he had seen men die, all kinds of men in all kinds of ways, but he had never learned to regard a man's passing as a trivial thing. Preston was dead, not from smallpox, not from fever, but from fear. It seemed such a useless way to cash in, even for a smuggler. Kiowa sighed, closed the dead man's eyes.

He passed the prisoners on his way to look for a shovel in Duncan's pack rig. Bobby Jack and Levi Skoda were asleep in their chains. A strange pair—the sad-faced little hunky and the beardless assassin. A strange and dangerous pair, Kiowa was thinking. And Fort Smith was a mighty long way from the Chickasaw Nation.

Not that he had any notion of trailing these killers clear to Arkansas. To Stonewall, maybe, like he'd first figured. From that point Wilkes and Skoda would be somebody else's problem.

: : : :

In a clearing beside the Washita Kiowa Jones dug steadily with the marshal's short-handled infantry trenching tool. A heavy dew had fallen during the night and the river bottom glistened and shimmered in the morning sun. Kiowa paused to wipe his sweaty face, noting how green and alive the country was, almost as if Nature were out-doing herself to make up for the two who were dead.

Bobby Jack Wilkes, in his usual sarcastic tone, call
"You want some help, cowboy? Just throw me the key
these leg irons and I'll show you how handy I can be."

Kiowa grinned sourly but said nothing. It was just as well that he aimed to cut loose from the prisoners in Stonewall; that pretty-faced killer was already beginning to ruffle Kiowa's feathers.

"How'd you like to be a rich man, cowboy?" Bobby Jack called.

"How'd you like to keep quiet awhile?"

The assassin laughed. "I mean it, Jones. The marshal told you about the thousand-dollar bounty, I guess."

Kiowa grunted.

"I'll double it, cowboy. Two thousand dollars. All yours, just for the takin'. All you have to do is throw me that key."

Kiowa climbed out of the grave and rested on the shovel. "No thanks. I wouldn't know what to do with that much money. But just for the sake of conversation, how'd you manage to raise two thousand dollars—in case I was a-mind to call you?"

Several seconds passed while Bobby Jack searched Kiowa's homely face for traces of greed. "Gettin' the money's easy. It's in the marshal's grain sack."

Kiowa's mouth twisted in a hard grin. "No thanks!"

For once the killer didn't try to be sarcastic; his expression was completely serious. "This is no trick, Jones. You don't have to give up the key until the money's in your hands."

For just a moment Bobby Jack had let his guard down, and Kiowa clearly saw the quiet but growing panic that lay behind those queer eyes. Swinging from old Izaac Parker's hanging machine didn't figure in Bobby Jack Wilkes's scheme of things. Well, Kiowa thought to himself, it's nice to know he's got nerves that can come unravelled, just like anybody else's. "Save your breath," he told the killer. "It's a long walk to Stonewall, and I want us to make it before dark."

Kiowa dragged Preston's body downstream to the clearing and buried the smuggler and marshal side by side. When the job was done, the graves filled, Kiowa stood beside the rounded mounds for a moment, feeling mean and angry and not understanding exactly why. "None of my doin'," he muttered under his breath. "They just got the fever and cashed in. No fault of mine."

But he felt older, and his shoulders seemed to stoop a little under an unseen and unwelcome weight. Methodically, he got together all the marshal's personal things, and Preston's too, and fed them to the fire. Clothing, bedding, trail equipment—everything except the gold, which stayed in the grain sack—even Duncan's saddle and good Navajo blanket went into the fire. The smoke, thick and black, boiled up in the bright spring morning, then settled over the river and hung there like a shroud.

"How about you, Skoda?" Kiowa asked the little hunky. "You feelin' all right?"

Levi Skoda smiled forlornly, nodding.

"Your head don't hurt? No pain in your gut?"

"Don't worry about me. The fever can't touch me. It's not in the cards."

"I'll ask you to remember that," Kiowa said dryly, "if you start puking your guts all over the prairie in a few hours."

Bobby Jack said, "You been thinkin' about my proposition, cowboy?"

"I thought about it. All that money would just land me in trouble. So I guess we'll go on to Stonewall, like I said."

The assassin shrugged and smiled, but a quiet rage watched Kiowa from those boyish eyes. "You're stupid, Jones. If you don't take the money, somebody else will. There's plenty men that wouldn't mind killin' a marshal, or a marshal's posseman, for the chance of pocketin' two thousand dollars. All the bounty hunters in the Territory will be on our trail—only it's not the bounty they'll be after. They know I'll double any price the law puts on my head. You think they'd go to all the trouble of takin' me clear to Arkansas, when they could make twice the money just by killin' you and turnin' me loose?"

Kiowa rubbed his chin thoughtfully, his mind still on the

new graves in the clearing. "How could anybody be on our trail? Nobody knows you've been captured."

Bobby Jack smiled, and this time it was real. "Some Indians know. Duncan stopped at an Apache farm school over in the Big Pasture. The word's out, Jones. And amongst bounty hunters news travels fast."

His expression blank, Kiowa turned to Skoda. "That right about stoppin' at the farm school?"

Skoda nodded.

"The Indians recognize Wilkes?"

The little hunky nodded again. "From circulars they'd seen at the trader's."

Two thousand dollars. A lot of men had been killed for a lot less. Still, with a little luck they could make Stonewall before dark, and there he would wash his hands of the business. Kiowa saddled his roan gelding and rode downstream to round up the marshal's horse and two pack animals. When he got back he removed the prisoners' leg irons and tightened the cuffs.

"I don't guess you gents would mind barebackin' it as far as the way station, would you?" Kiowa asked dryly.

Bobby Jack grinned his cynical grin, grabbed the mane of the marshal's saddle horse and waited for Kiowa to give him a leg up.

"I got myself a hunch, Jones. About all that smoke you made, burnin' the marshal's and Preston's plunder. How far you reckon smoke like that could be spotted in this country?"

Kiowa scowled. It hadn't occurred to him that the smoke might have been advertising their position to bounty hunters. Not, of course, that much could happen between here and the stage road.

"This is your last chance, cowboy," the assassin told him. "You can make yourself a rich man, or you can chance gettin' yourself ambushed on the trail. Which is it goin' to be?"

For an answer, Kiowa grabbed the killer's foot and boosted him to the animal's back. "How many times do you have to be told, Wilkes? The marshal was dead set on gettin' you to Smith, and I guess that's the way it's goin' to be."

The assassin's smiling mask slipped badly. For an instant hate, naked and deadly, contorted the boyish face. Kiowa met the look with bland unconcern, then turned and boosted Levi Skoda to the back of a pack horse.

CHAPTER THREE

THEY TRAVELLED EAST, leaving the meandering Washita behind them. By noon they were no more than an hour's ride from the stage road and maybe another three hours from the town of Stonewall, if it could be called a town. Kiowa had passed this way before and knew the place to be a typical Nations settlement, the stage office and operator, the handful of traders who would always do business on the outer fringes of the law.

The trip this far had been peaceful. No sign of bounty hunters. Near midday they stopped to rest the horses, and Kiowa built a fire and boiled some coffee from the dead marshal's supplies. A few more hours and it would be over; the responsibility of the prisoners would be somebody else's.

He should have felt relieved that everything was going so well. But there was something in the air, something unseen and unheard, but there all the same. Kiowa could smell it, the way an experienced lead steer could smell a pack of big grey lobos maybe four, five miles away.

Another thing—Bobby Jack Wilkes hadn't said a dozen words since leaving the plague camp. That wasn't like Wilkes—he enjoyed talking, playing on a man's nerves, uncovering and savouring all the bright subtleties that lay between normal caution and naked fear. But now he had pulled into himself, almost as if he were listening to sounds that no one else could hear.

They hunkered, the three of them, around the feeble cow-chip fire. They shredded whanglike jerky with their teeth and chewed until their jaws ached, washing the dried meat down with gulps of muddy coffee. Levi Skoda's eyes were narrow and watchful and his hand kept going to his shirt front, fingering the cards in his pocket. Kiowa had loosened the prisoners' cuffs but hadn't taken them off, and Bobby Jack began to curse fitfully as the chains got in the way of his eating.

"Goddammit, Jones, can't you unlock these things while we eat? And is that the best fire you can build?"

Suddenly the killer reached to one side, scooped green grass in both hands and dumped it on the fire. Instantly, Kiowa was on his feet, kicking the fire in all directions. "When I'm ready for smoke talk," he snarled to Wilkes, "I'll let you know."

Bobby Jack flushed. Then he grinned faintly, shrugged his shoulders, but said nothing.

They mounted and rode through the afternoon, across the rolling Red Beds of the Chickasaw Nation. Timber was heavy along the creek bottoms, but on the clay plains there was little plant life except for the grass. Tall blue-stem and lush grama, grass that would cure in the fall for winter feeding, grass that cattle would grow sleek and fat on, if they had the chance. Grass to set an old Panhandle cowman's mouth to slavering, and not a cow on it except for the small bunches of beef or dairy cattle that belonged to the Chickasaw farmers. Word had it that Texas cowmen were beginning to lease grass on the lower Washita, but Kiowa hadn't seen any sign of it.

The sight of so much good grazing land going to waste was enough to set any cowman to thinking, even a common, unrooted puncher like Kiowa Jones. He tried to figure it out. What did the Indians want with so much land that they didn't use? Why didn't the cowmen—the old-time fire-eaters like Goodnight or Loving or King—just drive their stock across the big Red and let that be the end of it? Who was to stop them?

The thought process, never easy, was especially painful to some men who, like Kiowa Jones, didn't go at it often enough to quite get the hang of it. At the moment all he could see was all that grass with no stock on it, and all he could feel was a certain troublesome but unfocused anger. He wanted to blame the Indians, but it wasn't that simple. The Katy Railroad was already a fact in the eastern part of the Territory, and rumour had it that the Santa Fé would soon start building down from Arkansas City. There was talk of boomers and throwing the Territory open to settlers. That would be the end of the grass. Homesteaders with their big sodbusting ploughs would take care of that.

Times were changing—that was the trouble—and not the cattle kings nor the Indians nor Kiowa Jones could stop it.

Kiowa clawed at his bristling chin. Struggling as he was with the unpleasant notion that time, and a free-and-easy way of living, were slipping away from him, and he could no more hold it than he could hog-tie an old wrinkled-horn bull with darning thread—occupied as he was with such deep and powerful thoughts, he clear forgot about his two prisoners.

He should have heard the grunt of the dead marshal's horse as Bobby Jack Wilkes kneed the animal alongside Kiowa's roan. But he was too busy worrying about what he would do when the last of the free range was gone and he became trapped in the tangle of nester fences.

He should have been warned by the nearby rattle of the assassin's cuff chains. But at that particular moment Kiowa Jones was wondering if he ought to forget about Caldwell and make for the New Mexico country, or maybe Arizona, where the spaces were bigger and harder to get a fence around.

He should have heard the breath whistling between Bobby Jack's clinched teeth the instant before the blow fell. As a matter of fact, Kiowa did hear it. But by that time it was too late.

Bobby Jack, hands raised high, hands clinched in a double fist, brought the heavy cuffs down on the back of Kiowa's neck. A star burst in Kiowa's labouring brain. The rolling plains tilted steeply and he found himself falling. No amount of clawing at saddle leather could break the fall, although he did manage, instinctively, to kick free of the stirrups.

Startled, the roan shied, then bolted. Kiowa Jones struck the hard clay sod with his shoulder, rolling with the fall. Instinct again. Or the hard, bone-breaking experience that a working cowhand gains over the years. Numbed but not unconscious, Kiowa grabbed awkwardly for his revolver, which he usually regarded as an item of apparel rather than a weapon. As a matter of convention he wore it when travelling and had become used to the solid weight on his hip, but it had been two years since he had fired it, accidentally, and almost as long since he had bothered to clean the cartridges or run a patch through the well-pitted barrel.

Lying on his back in the short grass, Kiowa dragged the .45 from its holster. Hurriedly he aimed at the assassin, jerked the trigger and snapped. A bad cartridge. Bobby Jack raked Duncan's horse with his heels. The nervous animal pounded away at a gait that would have carried the killer well out of pistol range in a matter of seconds.

Kiowa made a hard, bitter decision. Knowing that there was little or no chance of hitting Wilkes, he aimed at the larger target, the horse. It set his teeth on edge, but he held the revolver steady in both hands and gently squeezed the trigger instead of jerking it. The horse stumbled, then crashed to the ground, head over tail, the horse going one way, rider the other.

Drunkenly, Kiowa dragged himself to his feet and staggered toward the motionless rider. Only then did it occur to him that Levi Skoda had stayed out of it, hadn't made a move or a sound. Kiowa hesitated, eyeing that emotionless face with suspicion.

"What's the matter with you, Levi? You don't like the notion of makin' a break for it?"

Skoda lifted one dark eyebrow and shrugged. "I'm goin' to die anyway; nothin' can change that."

Snorting, Kiowa limped back, grabbed the lead rope, bringing the little hunky and the pack animal with him.

The horse was dead, not from Kiowa's bullet, which had only creased the animal's rump, but from a broken neck caused by the fall. Kiowa touched the glossy neck and shook his head. It was a sad day when a good horse had to die because of the likes of a Bobby Jack Wilkes.

The young killer was beginning to groan. Kiowa rolled him over with the toe of his boot. "Get up, Wilkes. You ain't hurt."

" When I fell, I think I broke my back. I can't move my legs."

" You better learn," Kiowa told him coldly. " You just ran out of horses, and it's still a long walk to Stonewall."

The killer was a boy again, young, bewildered, helpless. But smart enough not to let Kiowa see directly into those queer eyes.

" I swear it, Jones. I can't move my legs."

Kiowa scratched his jaw and fixed Bobby Jack with an icy grin. " So you can't move your legs. How do they feel?"

" Numb," Bobby Jack said weakly. " They can't feel a thing."

Kiowa's grin widened. " Then it won't make any difference."

". . . What do you mean?"

" A stingin' scorpion just crawled down your boot. But if you can't feel in your legs, it's nothin' to worry about."

The young assassin snarled, sat up and began tugging at both boots. The act was impulsive, involuntary, and almost immediately Bobby Jack realized that he had been tricked. With an effort he controlled his rage and once again assumed the boyish tone. " All right, Jones. You win." He held out his chain-linked hands. " How about helpin' me up?"

" Get up yourself." Kiowa was learning that words and intent were two different things. He had made a hammer-headed play and this time, through chance, had won; the next time Lady Luck might be sitting on Bobby Jack's side of the table. From here to Stonewall he meant to keep the killer always in his sights.

Trailing bridle reins had discouraged the roan's dash for the Texas border. The gelding had pulled up and was eyeing the human critters nervously from what it considered a safe distance. Kiowa shackled Bobby Jack's legs, hobbled Skoda's pack nag and went after the roan. When he came back he tied a lead rope to the killer's cuff chains and made the other end fast to his saddle-horn.

" Look here, Jones," the youth complained. " I can't go walkin' all the way to Stonewall."

"Be glad it ain't to Fort Smith," Kiowa said grimly, unlocking the leg irons.

The sun was half-way between straight up and the rolling horizon to the west. With a little luck, they could still make Stonewall before dark.

But this wasn't to be Kiowa's lucky day. A searing, bee-shaped bullet burned a small hole in the afternoon, just above Kiowa's head, missing his battered but prized Stetson by a matter of inches. A giveaway plume of black powder smoke drifted up from a grassy knoll. Bounty hunters.

Kiowa heard himself cursing hoarsely, eloquently. "Get on behind the hunky!" he yelled at Bobby Jack.

The assassin was shaking his head, grinning widely. "'Fraid I can't do it, Jones. The way you got me chained up."

Another bullet whistled down the grassy slope and dropped the pack horse. Kiowa hauled on the frightened roan, leaned out of the saddle and shoved his .45 in the assassin's face. His thumb jerked the hammer back. The double metallic click was surprisingly loud in the instant of silence. "Now!" he hissed as his finger started squeezing the trigger.

Bobby Jack saw the fingers, saw the stubborn thrust of the cowhand's jaw, saw the recklessness of a man who had been pushed as far as he intended to go. "All right!" the killer said quickly. No sense standing there and getting himself killed just to prove his nerve to an ignorant cow nurse.

A voice from the knoll was yelling: "Set steady. All of you. All we want's the bounty prisoner."

Bobby Jack raised his hands to Skoda. The little hunky grabbed them and hauled Wilkes up to the pack animal's sagging back. It seemed to take a lot of time. Kiowa snarled curses at the two men while he wheeled the roan, throwing off the dead pack horse's lead rope.

The voice from the knoll yelled again. "You can't run, Marshal! You haven't got a chance!"

They didn't know that Duncan was dead. Maybe that was good, maybe not. Time—maybe the next couple of seconds—would tell. Kiowa grabbed the remaining lead rope and pulled hard on the pack nag's halter. A second bounty hunter yelled something and another bullet burned down the green incline, snapping a dime-sized piece of leather from the cantle of Kiowa's saddle. That was no warning shot; they were shooting to kill.

Reluctantly, the pack nag began to move, shifting clumsily into a splay-footed lope that rattled the teeth of its riders. Bobby Jack, cursing wildly as more bounty hunter bullets began to fly, grabbed frantically at Skoda's neck, and Skoda had both hands locked in the animal's mane. Kiowa glanced back over his shoulder, too intent on keeping the animals moving to mind the shooting. He didn't like the looks of their chances. There were at least two bounty hunters, and it wouldn't take much manœuvring on these rolling plains to work out a deadly pattern of cross fire.

Kiowa felt a big emptiness where his guts were supposed to be, a cold emptiness, like a north wind moaning through a deep canyon. This business of dodging Winchester messengers wasn't the thing he was cut out for or trained for, and he wanted no part of it. What was he trying to prove, anyway? What did these prisoners mean to him, seeing as how he never had any notions of collecting the bounty? "Must be gettin' weak between the ears!" he growled under his breath as another bullet nicked the ear of the frantic roan.

"Be good enough for me," he grumbled angrily, "if them bushwhackers picked me right out of the saddle. What I ought to do is stop right here and tell 'em, 'All right, boys, they're your prisoners. You're welcome to 'em, I don't want no part of 'em.' That's what I ought to do. What I *would* do, if Kiowa Jones had the gumption a muley cow was born with!"

Folks that knew him would never lead you to believe that Kiowa Jones was a curly wolf or anything like it—on the other hand, he couldn't be called cold-footed either. It was just that he didn't take to dying at this particular time. Then, with blood-chilling suddenness, the luck of Kiowa Jones took a turn for the better—in a manner of speaking.

A cut-bank—a sheer drop of eight to ten feet—loomed directly in front of him. The roan saw it before Kiowa did and tried to avoid it, but the animal's momentum kept it going to the very edge and then down. For the second time that day Kiowa kicked free of the stirrups and dived out of the saddle. It was a long way down and a bone-shattering landing at the base of the reed clay bank. The roan fell with a sickening impact, and just behind came the pack nag and the two prisoners, Skoda still clutching double handfuls of mane and Bobby Jack Wilkes scorching the air with Gatling gun profanity.

The pack animal screamed as it hit the ground and lay kicking. The roan was motionless, dead, its head twisted back at a crazy angle and a bright froth of blood around the bit chain.

Kiowa's left shoulder was numb, and a good deal of skin and pants material was missing from the same side, but all his bones seemed to have held together. Bobby Jack Wilkes was on his hands and knees, blubbering in helpless rage like some young, tough brush bull that had just come under the castrating knife. Levi Skoda lay motionless a few feet from the kicking pack horse.

Painfully, Kiowa dragged himself to his knees. Cutbanks. The curse of trail drives. The subject of nightmares for all drovers, along with stampedes. Kiowa looked up at the sheer red wall and wondered how any of them had lived.

All of them hadn't. One horse dead, and the other one would have to be shot. And Skoda still hadn't moved.

Groggily, Kiowa pawed for his holster and found it empty. He began searching for the revolver before doing anything else, finding it at last near the pack horse, even dirtier than usual but still in one piece. Dimly, he recalled the bounty hunters. They could be expected to close in fast, like plain wolves finishing off a sick calf. That needed thinking about. But his head hurt, and too many things were crowding his mind and it was hard to get them straightened out. It was then that he saw Bobby Jack making for the dead roan and the battered Winchester in the saddle boot.

Kiowa heard himself saying, almost offhandedly, "That's far enough, Wilkes." He was surprised that his voice was so steady after what had just happened. The young killer blinked, holding one hand to his bloody nose. Apparently he was surprised too.

"Jones, you're goin' to need my help. Bounty hunters ain't particular who they shoot. You don't expect they'll let you go, do you?"

Kiowa raised the revolver and aimed it at Bobby Jack's head. "Get away from that rifle. Go over and see if there's anything you can do for the hunky."

Bobby Jack sneered. "You think you can hold off two scalp hunters?"

"I can try." He came in a little closer, but not so close that the assassin could see the clay dirt that clogged the cylinder.

The killer grinned, but with him it was an expression of hatred. "Have it your own way, cowboy. But before nightfall you'll be wolf bait, and I'll be free."

Levi Skoda began to groan. Bobby Jack limped over to him but did nothing to help, only stood there, looking first at Skoda and then at Kiowa, grinning. Kiowa hobbled over to the dead roan, slipped the rifle out of the boot but didn't try to peel his rig. Time enough for that later. If there was a later. He moved over to the hurt pack nag, looked for a moment into those big liquid eyes swimming in pain, then he placed the Winchester muzzle behind the animal's ear and fired.

Kiowa straightened, watching the prisoners. He had never killed a man, didn't know what it was like, but if it was any worse than killing horses he didn't want any part of it.

There was a sound of hooves in the distance—the bushwhackers were moving in to see how much mopping up they'd have to do. Kiowa got the leg irons out of the pack rig and motioned Bobby Jack against the cut-bank.

The killer was resigned but unworried. He sat with his back against the clay bank while Kiowa fastened the irons. "Have your fun, Jones. You've got just about five minutes to enjoy yourself, the way I figure it."

Kiowa shot him a bitter look. "We'll see, Wilkes." He knelt beside Levi Skoda and briefly studied the little hunky's face. "You feelin' all right?"

Skoda grimaced as he tried to sit up. Then Kiowa saw that Skoda's left leg was bent out at a crazy angle, and his stomach dropped. Not much chance of outrunning the bushwhackers or anybody else with a cripple on his hands, and everybody afoot. He glanced back at the cut-bank. Looked like this was where he'd have to make his stand. He pushed his hat back and wiped his forehead, faintly surprised to find that he was sweating heavily. He began to realize that he was scared—plenty good and scared—maybe more scared than he had ever been before.

Bobby Jack laughed softly. "Don't work up such a lather, cowboy. You don't want to live for ever, do you?"

"Shut up!" Kiowa snarled. That wasn't such a good sign. His control was beginning to slip. He was letting the assassin get under his skin. He wiped his face on his sleeve, then, self-consciously, jerked his hat down on his forehead. "Grit your teeth," he told Skoda. "I've got to drag you over to the cut-bank."

Kiowa began to tug. Skoda's face went as pale as suet but he didn't make a sound. He lay back against the red clay, gulping air.

"You all right, Skoda?"

". . . Sure . . ."

"I'll take a look at the leg later. Right now I'm a little crowded for time."

The hunky surprised him with a taut, blue-lipped grin, then, almost casually, slumped forward in a dead faint.

Kiowa noticed the silence that had suddenly fallen on the prairie. The bounty hunters had left their horses and were coming in on foot. That meant that they were getting close—too close for comfort.

"Marshal, you hear me?"

The voice came from above and to the right.

"Be sensible, Marshal. We got nothin' against you; all we want's the prisoner."

That was another voice, smoother, more experienced than the first, and it came from the left. Cross fire. The pattern was as obvious as it was deadly.

There was a spell of silence, maybe three or four minutes

of it; the bushwhackers made for opposite ends of the cut-bank. Kiowa used the time to study his position, noting first the heavy sod overhang at the top of the cut-bank. That at least eliminated the possibility of attack from above. And the pack nag that Skoda had been riding had fallen only a few yards away and could be used as a breastworks of sorts. Well, Kiowa tried to tell himself, at least it was better than trying to make a stand in the open.

But the place had one serious and probably fatal draw-back. It offered no way out, except forward, into the cross fire.

He was sweating again. And Bobby Jack Wilkes was grinning. Kiowa loaded the short-barrelled .44-40, then dug some of the clay and grass out of the revolver and hoped that it would fire at least a few times before exploding.

"You look worried, Jones," Bobby Jack said with obvious pleasure.

Kiowa turned and looked at the assassin with some of the cool stubbornness that backed up his spells of nerves. "Just thoughtful," he drawled. "I'm worried about you, Wilkes. Your future don't look so good to me."

The assassin looked startled. "*My* future?"

"All right, *ours*." Kiowa shrugged. "If this is where they bury me, it's where they bury you. You don't guess I'd just cash in and let you go, do you?"

For some unaccountable reason, the notion that this cow-hand might be capable of killing him in cold blood, if the bushwhackers started making it too hot, was a new and unpleasant idea for Bobby Jack. He had carefully noted Kiowa's near-criminal carelessness and ineptness with guns. Another thing—Kiowa's sickish reluctance to shoot the pack nag had not been wasted on the assassin. Clearly, such a man had little stomach for killing. Still. . . . Involuntarily, Bobby Jack lifted his cuffed hands and touched his own moist forehead. Still . . . some men played a reckless hand when they had their last chip on the table. Was Kiowa Jones such a man?

Kiowa, with a wide, mirthless grin, turned away and let the young killer stew. As for himself, he didn't know if he'd be capable of a cold-blooded killing. The next few minutes ought to tell. In the meantime it would be something for Bobby Jack to chew on.

"Marshal . . .!"

The scalp hunters were back. They had made their way down to the bottom of the jump-off, but, for the present, were staying out of sight. Kiowa lay on his belly, peering cautiously over the rump of the dead pack horse.

"Maybe we can strike a deal, Marshal." This from the soft-spoken one, over to Kiowa's right. The cool, experienced one with the syrupy conviviality of a back-country undertaker. "Not, of course, that you're in any position to deal," he went on conversationally. "But live and let live, I always say. Ain't that right, Jelly?"

Jelly, out of sight on Kiowa's left, laughed explosively. He sounded younger, meaner, tougher than the other bounty hunter—but not half so dangerous.

"What about it, Marshal?" the first one asked. "You favour a deal?"

"What kind?"

"Turn Wilkes over to us. That's all there is to it. We get Wilkes and you get away scot-free."

"Don't sound like much of a deal to me. My prisoner, with a thousand dollars on his head."

"That's one way of lookin' at it," the bounty hunter admitted. "But you'll never collect that reward, Marshal. Word's out about Wilkes; it's all over the Territory. Why, three different parties set out from Stonewall alone this mornin' when the stage brought the news."

Kiowa's stomach shrank until it felt like a hard, cold bullet in his gut. That took care of Stonewall. In Kiowa's over-active imagination he could see bounty hunters swarming like ground squirrels all over the prairie, and especially around Stonewall. He had a prisoner that was too dangerous to hold and even more dangerous to let go, so it seemed.

Not for an instant did Kiowa believe that these two bushwhackers would let him go, once they got their hands on the assassin. They would kill him without a qualm, just as Bobby Jack himself would kill him if he got the chance.

"You thought it over, Marshal?"

"Nothin' to think about, mister. The minute I step in the open, you'll shoot me. I'll just stay where I am, if it's all the same to you. So go ahead, try to get me in a cross fire. But you have to step in the open yourselves for that. And when the shootin' starts remember that Wilkes is right here beside me and he's no more bulletproof than I am—in case you had a notion of making a deal with him."

Bobby Jack shot a hot, cat-eyed glance at Kiowa. This thing wasn't working out to be as simple as it had first seemed. These unforeseen hazards were making him nervous. And this cowhand that he had been taking so lightly was showing a back-to-the-wall stubbornness that might well get them both killed.

"I was hopin' you'd be reasonable about this, Marshal," the bushwhacker sighed.

Jelly, from the left, snarled impatiently. "That's enough gab, Morgan. I say shoot him out of there and be done with it."

The first one, the one called Morgan, grunted to himself. Grunted and must have shrugged a shrug of resignation. Nothing risked, nothing gained. Then, on what must have been a prearranged signal, both men dived out of niches in the clay bank and blasted the area with their saddle guns.

This was the thing that Kiowa had braced himself for, but he had not expected such violence. When they had shot at him the first time it had been a chilling experience hearing the slugs of lead scorching the clear air around his head. This was something else. He had known cross fire as a theory; now he knew it as all the violence of a stampede concentrated to the size of a handful of bullets. Violence that slammed into the pack nag carcass, ripping it to pieces, spattering his face with gore, stunning him so that he couldn't fire a single shot in return.

Then it was over. Kiowa lay with his face in the clayey sod, his mouth cottony, his throat constricted until breathing was just barely possible. He was not alone. Bobby Jack Wilkes, his eyes tightly closed, gouged at the red clay until his fingers were bloody, burrowing like a mole in a sand hill.

Only Levi Skoda remained unaffected and untouched by the withering fire. The little hunky, recovered from the faint, sat bolt upright against the dirt bank, absolutely sure in his mind that these bushwhackers' bullets could not kill him, because he was destined to die on the gallows at Fort Smith, and it could be no other way. The tarot had told him so.

CHAPTER FOUR

A GOOD DEAL OF TIME, counted in seconds, must have passed before Kiowa steadied himself to peer over the tail end of the pack animal. Nothing but prairie ahead of him. Grassy knolls, valleys, gullies, scattered clumps of brush and tall grass. No bushwhackers. But there was a voice.

"That was just a taste, Marshal. You ready to listen to our proposition now, or do you want some more cross fire?"

It was the smooth talker, the one called Morgan, somewhere out front to Kiowa's right. He couldn't see where. But in some gully or draw, or behind some bush or low-lying formation of red sandstone, they were out there, waiting. This was their business, killing from ambush, and they were good at it.

"You hear me, Marshal?"

"He hears, all right!" Bobby Jack yelled, suddenly finding his voice. "And he ain't no marshal, just a common cowhand."

Snarling, Kiowa flipped over on his left side, swung the Winchester with his right hand, like a Comanche swinging a war axe, and knocked the assassin sprawling. "Another play like that and you'll never live to see that hangin' machine at Fort Smith! You hear me, Wilkes?"

Bobby Jack raised himself to one elbow, thick, red blood dripping from his mouth. There was a broken-glass glitter in those queer eyes. "Before the day's over you'll pay for that, cowboy."

"Nothin' comes free in this life," Kiowa grated. "Just mind what I told you."

Once more the voice of the bounty hunter seemed to float up from the green sod. "A cowhand. Well now, that's right interestin'." He sounded pleased, relieved and vaguely amused. "All right, cowhand, what's your play goin' to be?"

Looked like he didn't have any say-so in the matter. You bet your stack and took the cards as they fell. Kiowa sighed heavily, heartily wishing that he was back riding line or greasing windmills.

Then, as abruptly as before, he found himself on the sharply focused point of the cross fire. It was still a long way from pleasant, but it wasn't as bad as it had been the first time. Firing over the pack animal's neck, Kiowa even got off three shots of his own, spotting Morgan's smoke floating up from a shallow gully.

It gave the bushwhackers something to think about. Getting Wilkes wasn't going to be as easy as they had figured. Not that it couldn't be done. It would just take a little time, and maybe they'd have to run a few more chances than they would have liked.

No more talk from the scalp hunters. No sound or sight. Several minutes dragged by and Kiowa began to itch with impatience. What were they scheming? What were they waiting on?

He glanced back over his shoulder, and Bobby Jack, dabbing at his bloody mouth, shot him a graveyard smile. He *knew* what they were waiting on. He and the bounty hunters were apples off the same tree; they thought alike. He knew what they had in store for Kiowa, and it pleased him.

"What's the matter, cowboy? You gettin' a little edgy?"

"Just keep your mouth shut," Kiowa told him.

The assassin laughed softly. "Sure. I'll be quiet. I want to concentrate on you, Jones. I want to watch you sweat." He glanced up at the deep blue sky. "But take it easy, Jones. They're not goin' to kill you now. Not quite yet. About two hours from now . . . that's when they'll kill you."

Kiowa scowled. The assassin seemed so cocksure, he must

know what he was talking about. But it didn't make sense; why would they lie out there doing nothing, just waiting?

Time dragged. About an hour had passed, according to Kiowa's calculations, and still no sign of the bushwhackers. Maybe they had pulled out. Maybe they had decided that even two thousand dollars wasn't worth the risk. But that was wishful thinking, and Kiowa knew it.

Bobby Jack said nothing. With that killer's smile on his boyish face, he kept his gaze fixed on Kiowa. Skoda sat with his back against the cut-bank, with sickness in those dark eyes.

"How you doin', Skoda?"

The little hunky shrugged.

"Don't move that leg any more than you have to. I'll have a go at settin' it, soon's things settle down here."

The dark, hatchet-like face of Levi Skodaschinski turned to Kiowa, and he nodded. Bobby Jack's smile widened. He glanced from the prairie to the setting sun to Kiowa. Every few minutes his gaze would follow the same pattern. What did he see out there that amused him so?

The sun was sinking low in the west. Kiowa shaded his eyes and peered cautiously over the carcass of the dead pack animal. Suddenly it came to him. Now he knew what the bounty hunters were waiting on. The sun. In a few minutes it would be just right, and they would come after him, out of the sun.

Bobby Jack had known all along. Now he watched Kiowa's face with glee. "How do you like it now, cowboy? Did you ever try to shoot somebody comin' at you out of the sun?"

Kiowa, with an ache in his gut, squinted into the dazzling light. He might as well be blind, for all the good his eyes were going to do him.

Maybe it was the thought of blindness that sharpened his hearing. The silence of the prairie was disturbed for a moment by the high-pitched squeak of an ungreased wagon wheel. It was faint and far away, but he was sure that he had heard it. Bobby Jack hadn't, and neither had Skoda. Tensely, Kiowa tuned his hearing to the wagon-wheel pitch.

But it didn't come again. He glanced up at the sky and saw a soaring black shadow against the blue, and soon he had convinced himself that it had been the distant scream of a hawk that he had heard.

The sun was sinking steadily lower. Silently Kiowa Jones cursed himself for his own stupidity, for stopping at a smallpox camp, for getting himself mixed up with lawmen and assassins and sad-eyed little gipsy gamblers.

The sun slipped another fraction of an inch closer to the western horizon. Kiowa rested his rifle on the neck of the dead horse. The minutes ticked away. He tried not to look at the sun. But that's where the killers would come from; he had to look.

Then, after what seemed a long wait, they were coming, right out of the circle of blinding light. Kiowa could hear them coming at an easy trot, but he could see nothing, not even the sights of his own rifle. A short piece from the cutbank the bushwhackers stopped and began firing, leisurely shooting Kiowa's flesh-and-blood breastworks to pieces.

A bushwhacker bullet nicked Kiowa's ancient Stetson and snatched it from his head. In a sudden blind, helpless fury, he staggered to his feet and fired as fast as he could lever cartridges into the Winchester. In his rage, he threw the rifle down when it was empty and started for his tormentors with his bare hands.

He stumbled, fell sprawling a few yards in front of the cutbank. He tried to climb to his feet, amazed when he made it, expecting to be caught and riddled in the deadly cross fire. The sound of shooting was confused; it seemed to be coming from behind him instead of in front of him. In his blindness he had lost his sense of direction.

He wheeled awkwardly and blundered in the opposite direction, and this time tripped over the dead pack horse and fell again.

The shooting had stopped. Kiowa didn't understand what had happened, but his hearing, still sharply tuned, caught the sound of horses beating a hurried retreat to the west. The bounty hunters? That didn't seem likely. But who? And why?

A hundred match-head suns danced behind his eyes. He kept them tightly closed for several seconds, then opened them slowly, blinking as the red wall of the cut-bank came into blurred focus.

Then a voice—a woman's voice, cool, businesslike and unruffled—called, " Just stand steady, mister, till I get a better look at you."

Startled, Kiowa squinted hard at the top of the cut-bank where a woman was peering down at him over the long barrel of an ancient Winchester repeater, a model '63 if Kiowa could trust his misty vision. He hadn't been as confused as he had thought. There *had* been rifle fire at his back.

" Ma'am," he said, with all the gravity he could muster, " I don't know who you are or why you did it, but I'm sure obliged for your help."

" Miss," she snapped at him. " Miss Amilia Rathmore." She lowered the rifle a few inches, made a snorting sound and asked, " You a lawman?"

" No, ma'am. . . . I mean, these two prisoners, they belonged to a lawman, a government deputy by the name of Duncan. But he died. I just kind of got left with them." He couldn't tell much about her. A sunbonnet hid her face, a shapeless grey print dress concealed any figure she might have had. She could have been any age between twenty and fifty. Kiowa remembered the wheel squeak that he had heard, or thought he had heard. It must have been this woman's wagon.

" Stand steady," she told him again. For a moment she disappeared, then Kiowa saw her circling the far end of the cut-bank. Now, on the same level, she came toward him, that long-barrelled Winchester still at the ready. " Who were those two men?" she asked. " And why were they so set on killing you?"

Kiowa tried to explain about the prisoners and the price on Wilkes's head and the double-bounty price that Wilkes himself was putting on his freedom. Amilia Rathmore eyed the prisoners suspiciously. " That man's hurt," she said, indicating Skoda.

" Yes, ma'am. . . . I mean, his leg got broke when we went

off the cut-bank. A while back I thought I heard a wagon. Would that of been yours?"

Miss Rathmore nodded. "A light wagon and a reasonably good team. But I have no intention of hauling your prisoners for you, if that's what you had in mind."

Kiowa had the uneasy feeling that she was reading his mind. She pushed her sunbonnet back and looked again at the prisoners. She had about the kind of face that Kiowa had expected. Eyes that were blue and sharp but somehow distorted through the steel-rim spectacles perched like twin burning glasses on the bridge of her nose. Not much of a chin, but a wide, expressive mouth that chopped her words shorter than grass on a sheep range. One word pretty well summed up Amilia Rathmore: plain. Her hair was an indifferent brown, just a little lighter than a chestnut mare that Kiowa had owned once, and she wore it town-style, pulled severely back over her ears and done in a knot at the nape of her neck. Plain.

Kiowa resisted a sigh of disappointment. She wheeled without warning and fired a question. "What is your name, sir?"

"Jones. Kiowa Jones."

"That's a queer name. You don't look Indian."

"I ain't. My old man, my pa, he was a trader over at Fort Sill, so I was pretty much brought up with kids from the Plains tribes. The soldiers called me Kiowa."

She studied him from behind her thick lenses, then made a quick gesture with her left hand. "Those bounty hunters. They'll be back, I expect, if that young prisoner is as valuable as you say he is."

"He is," Kiowa said gravely. "And they will. Unless you might be willin' to give me a hand. I know, you said your wagon's not for haulin' prisoners, but you can see for yourself the hunky's in no shape to hoof it."

Her mouth came shut like a steel trap. She was already shaking her head. "I appreciate your situation, Mr. Jones, but what you suggest is out of the question. I'm bound for Tahlequah where the Cherokee Council has hired me to teach in their National Female Seminary. Can you imagine what the school officials would think if I arrived there with two prisoners, and murderers at that, in my wagon?"

Kiowa blinked and squinted at her. "You're goin' all the way to the Cherokee Nation, by yourself?"

She eased the spectacles down her slender nose and peered at him. "I am perfectly capable of looking after myself, Mr. Jones, as I am sure those two bounty hunters will agree."

"That reminds me. I don't guess you hit them, did you?" She sniffed primly. "I wasn't aiming to kill. I had no way of knowing what the commotion was about, but when I saw them shooting at you, with the sun at their backs . . ." With a flick of her hand she dismissed her part in the fray. "It seemed to me that they were taking unfair advantage of you, that's all."

Kiowa surprised both of them by grinning. "I guess you'll make it to Tahlequah all right." But Lord help the Cherokee schoolgirls at the seminary. "Thanks again for your help. I'll walk back to the wagon with you."

"That won't be necessary, Mr. Jones." She handled the rifle like a man, cradling it in the crook of her right arm. She nodded curtly, turned and started back up the slope toward the tapered end of the cut-bank. After a few steps she hesitated and glanced back. "I suppose I could help you set the prisoner's leg. It shouldn't take more than a few minutes."

Skoda's face was colourless, drawn with pain. Kiowa started cutting off the prisoner's boot and the little hunky sat bolt upright, gasping. "Here," Amilia Rathmore said, "give me that knife. Do you have any whisky?"

"This is Indian Territory," Kiowa said dryly. "It's worth a man's neck to be caught carryin' whisky in this country."

She merely smiled, removing the boot as neatly as peeling a Christmas banana. "There's a jug in my wagon—for medicinal purposes, understand. Up front under the seat. Please get it for me, Mr. Jones."

Kiowa shot her a sidelong glance. "All right, but watch out for Wilkes. He's a great one for play-actin' when there's an audience around."

Bobby Jack shot Kiowa a black look but said nothing. Amilia Rathmore merely grunted and began slitting Skoda's pants leg.

From the top of the cut-bank, Kiowa could fully appreciate the field of fire that Amilia Rathmore had used so well. With the aid of her hooded sunbonnet, and aiming down at a fairly sharp angle, she hadn't had the sun to plague her. Old Jelly and Morgan, the bushwhackers, must have felt as naked as skinned squirrels when she started cracking down on them with that Winchester.

The wagon was a light spring farm wagon, neatly rigged and packed. The team was well cared for, harness in good condition, but one of the axles needed grease. That small failing made Kiowa feel some better—it went to show that Amilia Rathmore was, after all, merely human.

The whisky was just where she had said it would be. Kiowa uncorked it, sniffed the heady bouquet of oak-aged corn liquor and swigged heartily from the neck of the jug. When he returned to the bottom of the cut-bank, Miss Rathmore took the jug, shook it and said coldly, "Anyhow, you didn't drink *all* of it. Here," she told Levi Skoda, dribbling the amber liquid into the hunky's mouth. It was then that Kiowa noticed Bobby Jack sulking, nursing an anger as black as the inside of the coalpits over in the Choctaw Nations. There was a long but shallow wound on the assassin's arm.

"What happened here?" Kiowa demanded.

For a moment Amilia Rathmore looked blank. Then: "Oh. There was some question in Mr. Wilkes's mind as to who should be in possession of this knife. You needn't worry. His wound is superficial."

"It wasn't him I was worried about," Kiowa drawled. "Maybe I should of been." His feeble humour went over her head.

"Please help me, Mr. Jones. Take his foot and pull slowly, with even pressure. . . ."

Between the two of them they set the broken bone with a minimum of fuss. Kiowa cut saplings and put the leg in splints. He tried not to worry about the bounty hunters. It wasn't easy. Jelly and Morgan hadn't struck him as the sort to knock off the job just because a woman had got the drop on them.

"That will do, I think," Amilia Rathmore said brusquely. She took up her jug and rifle. "Good day, Mr. Jones. I'm sorry I can't be of more help."

"It's almost sundown. You can't travel this country by night."

She smiled a superior kind of smile that Kiowa could soon learn to dislike with no trouble at all. "As long as there is a good moon I can travel very well, thank you. There's no time to spare—I've only two weeks to reach Tahlequah."

With effort Kiowa resisted the temptation to say something angry and foolish. You might as well argue with a muley cow as try to convince a hammerheaded woman. "Well, I guess I can't stop you. Do you know the way?"

"I have a map. Don't worry about me, Mr. Jones."

"No, ma'am," he told her, "I won't."

"Miss," she told him primly and a little defensively. "Good day, Mr. Jones."

"Good day, Miss Rathmore."

He watched her go, straight and proud as a Cheyenne war chief. After a while he heard the wagon start. That axle still needed greasing.

"A good woman," Levi Skoda said softly. "But foolish. Proud and foolish."

: : : :

It was not Levi Skoda's way to complain. He sat with his back against the cut-bank, his eyes closed, his thoughts his own. The ghost of Amabel, his wife—his dead wife—was with him. Amabel of the sweet-wine lips, the liquid eyes, the brazen laughter. How he ached for her and wished that she were alive, truly alive. And yet he knew that if the scene were to be acted out all over again, if she should somehow be brought back to life at this very moment, only to taunt him with her infidelity, then he would kill her exactly as he had done before.

Almost from the beginning the tarot had indicated a violent end for them. She, with the wild blood of Spanish gipsies in her veins, an outcast, an infamy to her own people. He, with his Slav gipsy mother and half-wild Cossack for a father. Too much hot blood, too much wildness. The last bad fruit of a diseased orchard . . . it couldn't have ended any other way. But Lord, how he ached for her.

He tried not to think of Amabel. He turned his mind to the Old Country, but there was little that he could remember. He had been quite young when he, his mother, and his mother's husband of the moment shipped from Odessa to New York, and then to Pennsylvania where his mother's husband worked in the coalpits. Soon Levi himself was descending daily into the pits, down in the bowels of the earth, to depths as black and frightening as the pits of *Il Diavolo*.

This was no kind of work for a young man whose namesake was Eliphas Levi. He left the pits and moved west to St. Louis where he learned, to his amazement, that a man could make a living of sorts simply by being expert with cards. Young Levi Skodaschinski could not remember the time when he had not been expert with the magical seventy-eight cards of the tarot. Mastering a common poker deck was child's play.

He worked the riverboats, making a living but not much more, for his heart was not in gambling. In his own mind, at least, he was a scholar; truly he was his mother's son, searching for the old truths. A scholar whose one book was the tarot, perhaps the only book to survive the flames that devoured the great library of the ancient Egyptians. All sorts of men came West in the '80s and Levi Skodaschinski's preoccupation with "hoodoo" cards was accepted with a minimum of curiosity. The pierced lobe of his left ear, from which a small gold ring had once swung, had long since grown over with scar tissue. With a wild thing's instinct for protective coloration, young Skoda adopted the Westerner's dress and speech, but wherever he went he was always referred to as "bohunk" or "hunky."

Young Skodaschinski didn't mind. A chameleon was still a lizard, no matter how hard he tried to look like a leaf or a twig or a piece of dappled shade. Until the time of Amabel his cards were the only things that mattered.

Amabel! Amabel! With his knife he had plumbed the rottenness of her heart, and her blood had gushed over his hand, hotter than bubbling lead, brighter than gipsy sashes. And she had cursed him as she fell. Aii! Aii! To the world he showed a high-cheeked, leathery, impassive mask, but his heart was black.

: : : :

For a time after the incredible rout of the bounty hunters Bobby Jack Wilkes sat in a stunned rage. The bunglers! Allowing a woman, a schoolteacher, to drive them off as easy as driving rabbits out of a turnip patch! A pair of gutless wonders! The young assassin at that moment could have gleefully killed both of them. But the rage reached its peak and began a measured retreat. Time enough to attend to gutless wonders . . . after he was free of shackles and wrist irons.

Jelly and Morgan would return. The lure of double bounty would bring them. Bobby Jack grinned viciously to himself. That cowhand, sticking his long nose into things that were none of his business. It was a pleasure to close his eyes and speculate on the many ways that a busybody like Jones could die. The knife, the gun, the fine, hand-braided rope. They all had their points. Once, down in Galveston, Bobby Jack had seen a little slant-eyed sailor kill a man with his bare hands. Whack, whack—just like that, right behind the ear the little slant-eye hit him, and the man had gone down like a sack of buckshot, with a broken neck. Bobby Jack had greatly admired the way the slant-eye had handled himself, and he had often wished that he had stayed around to learn how he had done it.

A man never learned too much in this business.

A thought, like a vulture's shadow, drifted across the assassin's mind. That old maid schoolteacher! If he'd only managed to get that knife from her, things would be some different by this time. Even a man with many varied and special talents usually prized one above all the others. Bobby Jack Wilkes had a special fondness for bright, shining blades.

The knife, except in cases of emergency, he liked to reserve for special people. And the more he thought about it the surer he was that Kiowa Jones deserved the knife. A fine steel edge drawn slowly, expertly across the throat. Bobby Jack grinned. He could almost see the look on the cowhand's face.

: : : :

Kiowa Jones was a man trapped by his own indecision. His chances of fighting off another bushwhack attempt were too long to be seriously considered. He hated the notion of staying here and probably dying here, and yet he couldn't quite make up his mind to leave. Always there had been a boss, a foreman, a ranch owner, somebody to tell him what to do. He'd never had much practice in making decisions on his own.

He stripped his dead gelding, mumbling angrily to himself. "What I ought to do is light out of here afoot. Like them scalpers said, I ain't the one they want, it's Wilkes. Just light out of here and turn Wilkes over to them. That's what I ought to do. I never asked to be no government marshal anyhow."

He eyed the setting sun, shining like a big brass gaboon on the western horizon. He kept an eye peeled for movement on the prairie, any kind of movement that might tip him off that Jelly and Morgan were back to claim their prize. Damn that Duncan, anyhow. What did he have to go and die for?

The problem of what to do about Skoda nagged at Kiowa. It was a hard thing, just walking off and leaving the little hunky sitting there with a busted leg to shift for himself.

Kiowa lugged his rig and equipment over to the cut-bank and Bobby Jack looked at him with those grinning coyote eyes.

"You look a little sweaty, cowboy. You wouldn't be worried old Jelly and Morgan'll come back, would you?"

Suddenly, with the help of the assassin's sneering question, Kiowa definitely decided against pulling out. "You just keep on talkin', Wilkes, and you'll talk yourself right in the middle of old Judge Parker's hangin' machine."

The assassin laughed. "You're dead, Jones. You just don't know it yet."

Kiowa squatted behind the dead pack horse, studying the prairie. They were out there somewhere pulling themselves together for another attack, but moving cautiously this time, making sure no one was on top of the cut-bank to surprise them. Suddenly Kiowa jumped to his feet, realizing why the prairie was so empty. He grabbed his rifle and headed for the far taper of the cut-bank.

In a horseman's awkward, hard-gaited lope, he reached the level of the prairie and threw himself face down in the grass. The bounty hunters had panicked, all right; they had been routed by a woman, but they hadn't been lying out on the prairie all this time, shaking in their boots. They had been swinging wide around the cut-bank, closing in on the side of the jump-off, to make double sure that Amilia Rathmore and her twenty-year-old Winchester weren't there to greet them. Kiowa breathed a deep sigh when he saw them crawling out of a grassy draw less than two hundred yards from the jump-off and about half of that from the muzzle of his own short-barrelled .44-40.

The sun was gone; the light was tricky, but at least Kiowa didn't have it in his eyes. Jelly and Morgan stood out sharply against the fading brilliance of the sky. Kiowa watched them over the sights of his Winchester. Full of confidence, the bushwhackers raised out of their crouch and moved on toward the jump-off.

Let them come a little closer. When he threw down on them he wanted them to see immediately that they were covered and that fighting would be suicidal. It would have been a simple thing to end it then and there—add a little extra pressure to the trigger, bring the hammer down on the rim-fire .44 calibre cartridge, and Jelly would be dead. Or Morgan.

But killing wasn't a thing to be decided on the whim of a moment; it was a sober thing, a last-resort thing, and Kiowa still held grimly to the notion that it could somehow be avoided. It was then that Morgan, the older one, the lean, hard, experienced one, came up short, seeing Kiowa in the grass. He wheeled with his carbine and fired from the hip.

Kiowa felt a twinge of disappointment. Somehow he had

expected something better from Morgan. Even a common cowhand knew that hip shooting was a poor way to stop trouble.

Jelly, a sleek young man wearing town clothes and short boots, also armed with a carbine, let out a startled yelp and began firing wildly. Kiowa gritted his teeth and cursed. A quiet solution to Jelly and Morgan wasn't in the cards. Morgan was already recovering from his surprise and was dropping to one knee, infantry fashion, taking that extra split second to aim.

The choice was out of Kiowa's hands. With Morgan already in his sights, Kiowa squeezed the trigger, winced a little as the hardwood stock slammed against his unprotected shoulder. The bounty hunter threw his head back, as if in amazement, took two awkward steps, then lost his balance and fell face down across his saddle gun.

Kiowa turned his attention to Jelly. He made a point of not looking back at Morgan.

Jelly, young and reckless, stared bug-eyed as his partner went down. Then, wild with rage, he charged at Kiowa, carrying the fight to point-blank range. Kiowa squeezed the trigger again. The Winchester snapped.

A cold finger raked up Kiowa's back. The much-abused weapon had jammed and the lever wouldn't eject the faulty cartridge. It seemed that he could almost feel Jelly's angry breath in his face. The young bushwhacker bared his teeth, pointed his carbine at Kiowa and fired as he ran.

Kiowa's long practice in dodging maddened old range cows came to his aid. With surprising speed, he flipped over on his left side, clawing for his revolver. One of Jelly's bullets tore a long, red wound in the clayey sod, in the spot where Kiowa had been an instant before. The bounty hunter was almost on top of him when Kiowa felt the revolver buck in his hand, heard the shocking bellow of the explosion, and saw once again that look of amazement in Jelly's face.

It was a lucky shot. Kiowa saw the small black hole appear just below Jelly's shirt pocket. Jelly came on for two or three steps, his mouth wide open, yelling without making a sound, like something out of a bad dream. At last he fell, no more than a dozen yards in front of Kiowa, fell and moaned, or perhaps it was only the sound of air forced from his lungs when he hit the ground. He didn't move. Jelly was as dead as his partner, and Morgan was as dead as they came.

A voice from the cellar of Kiowa's mind spoke sardonically. "Two shots, two hits, two men dead. Not bad shootin' for a cowhand." His stomach seemed to crowd into his throat and for one bad moment he was afraid that he was going to be sick. Maybe Morgan and Jelly hadn't been much, but they had been men, and he knew now that killing men was worse than killing horses. The thing he had done could never be undone. That was the thing about killing that made it so bad.

Slowly, Kiowa got to his feet, his aim and direction gone. He had a sudden urge to turn and walk away from the scene and make like it had never happened, make like he was the same Kiowa Jones that had ridden over from the Panhandle a few days before, with not a worry in his head.

Not much chance. That was something else about killing, he was learning. It worked both ways. The Kiowa Jones of a few days ago—or a few minutes ago, for that matter—lay as dead as Jelly and Morgan. It would take some time getting used to this other man who had lain out here on the prairie and, in a matter of seconds, had become a double killer.

From the foot of the cut-bank Bobby Jack Wilkes began yelling in glee. "Down here, boys! Get the keys out of the cowhand's pocket! Let me out of these chains, and you'll be rich men, both of you!"

Slowly, Kiowa Jones began to find his direction.

"The keys're in the cowhand's pocket, boys! All you got to do is unlock these irons. . . ."

Kiowa grabbed his Winchester, went a way along the cut-bank, then skidded down to the bottom. The assassin gaped. The colour drained from his face. It just didn't figure that one clumsy, ignorant ranch hand could beat two bounty hunters at their own game. Bobby Jack must have thought that he was seeing a ghost. Even Levi Skoda, who seldom showed what he was thinking, looked surprised.

Kiowa glared at them, racking his brain for just the right

words, cocky, brass-tipped, cynical. He wasn't just anybody now. He'd killed men.

But all he could think of to say was: " At least we won't be afoot, if I can round up the scalpers' horses."

CHAPTER FIVE

THE LINGERING PRAIRIE TWILIGHT turned the land black and the sky a muddy pink streaked with blood-poison red. Kiowa and the two prisoners chewed jerky at the bottom of the cut-bank.

" Least you could do is build a fire and make coffee," Bobby Jack said sourly.

Kiowa merely looked at him, sick of him, hating him, and not knowing what to do with him. Wanting to get rid of him, but fighting to hold him. It didn't make sense. Nothing about this business made sense. Like a rabbit caught in a Comanche snare—the harder he pulled to get away, the tighter he was caught.

" Look here, Jones——"

" Shut up," Kiowa told him coldly. " I don't want to listen to that loud mouth of yours to-night."

With a snarl, Bobby Jack hurled his cold jerky to the ground. For a while there was silence, and darkness came down on the prairie. Then, as he understood the cowhand's edginess, the assassin lay back in his chains and laughed to himself.

Morgan and Jelly were still where they had fallen. Kiowa hadn't touched them and couldn't seem to get himself started at the task of grave digging. Still, he knew that it wouldn't do to put the burying off too long, with the big grey lobos prowling these plains. The horses had been caught and picketed in the deep grass below the cut-bank. Supper, such as it was, had been drawn out as long as possible, until his squeamish stomach rebelled, and there was nothing else to keep him from the digging.

He rose to his feet and got the shovel out of the dead marshal's pack. Kiowa found a place near a scrubby thicket of redbud and blackjack and began to dig. He worked steadily, worked until sweat plastered his clothing to his body, and the touch of the night breeze was steely and clean. Working now, after his muscles had loosened, with a kind of machinelike efficiency, he planted the two bounty hunters in the narrow graves and covered their faces with their own bandannas.

Morgan—who was he? Did he have a family, wife, kids, home? Was there someone somewhere who would miss him, or maybe even mourn him? And Jelly, the young, reckless one who had raced headlong toward death, as though he just couldn't wait to meet it. Jelly who? Where had he come from, what was he doing with an old hand like Morgan?

Kiowa sighed, a sound with the weight of years behind it, and began filling the graves. When he finished he rested on the shovel, panting, dimly wondering if something more ought to be done or said, or if he ought to just walk off and let them rest. He decided to go. The things that were in his mind, Morgan and Jelly wouldn't know what he was talking about, even if they could hear him. Kiowa shouldered the shovel. That was when he heard the unmistakable squeak of an ungreased axle.

The wagon topped a dark knoll, rising boldly against the night-grey of the sky. Scowling, Kiowa moved toward it and called.

". . . Miss Rathmore?"

"Mr. Jones!" The sound of relief was in the woman's voice. She urged her team forward, toward the jump-off, where Kiowa waited. "I heard gunfire—or thought I did. Perhaps I was mistaken."

Kiowa, with a puzzled note in his voice, said, "No mistake, I guess. Old Morgan and Jelly, they had another go at me. But their luck played out."

"You drove them off?" She sounded surprised.

"Killed them. Like I said, their luck played out."

There was something in the way he said it. Amilia Rathmore peered down at him, studying the dim outline of his homely face. Then, after several seconds of silence, she reached under the wagon seat and handed down the whisky jug.

"What's that for?"

"Take it."

He took it without argument and swigged from the neck, grateful for the distracting fire that spread in his stomach, drinking steadily until his throat rebelled and he began to cough. He corked the jug and handed it back.

"It's an ugly thing, killing," she said impersonally, sliding the jug back under the seat. "I saw some of it when I was a young girl and the Quahadas were raiding over to the west, along the Canadian. Ugly. But there are times when it must be done."

Kiowa looked up at her. "You sure about that?"

She moved uncomfortably on the wagon seat, her face hidden in the hood of her sunbonnet. She decided to ignore the question. "Are you all right? I mean, you weren't wounded, were you?"

"I'm fine, Miss Rathmore." The warmth of the whisky spread through his body, making him a little lightheaded. "It surprises you, don't it, me comin' out on top of two bounty hunters? Well, it surprises me, too. But now that I think about it, old Morgan and Jelly never had a chance. I just yanked the trigger on that old Winchester and down they went. Let me tell you somethin', they was more surprised than anybody." He pushed his hat back and grinned, without a trace of mirth. "Just yanked the trigger, one, two, like that, and down they went. You ever kill anybody, Miss Rathmore?"

". . . No." In a strange, finely drawn voice.

"I don't recommend it. It don't go down the way you might think. It sticks in your gullet, hard as a bullet, heavy as a Cheyenne biscuit. Tell me somethin'," he said, abruptly changing directions. "How come you turned around and came back here? You claimed to be in a hurry to get to that Cherokee seminary, the last I saw of you."

She hesitated. Then, without seeing her face, Kiowa knew that she was returning his humourless grin. "Perhaps I returned for the same reason you stuck with the prisoners and wouldn't turn them over to the bounty hunters."

Kiowa puzzled that in his mind for a few seconds before replying: "I rounded up the bushwhackers' horses, which beats bein' afoot by a considerable piece, but it don't help much with the hunky. I don't guess you had it in mind to let Skoda ride in your wagon, did you?"

Clearly, the same question had been in Amilia Rathmore's mind for some time, and she had been holding back with an answer. "Well, his leg *is* broken, and he must be in considerable pain. I suppose I could haul him as far as Stonewall."

Kiowa shook his head. "It won't do. For one thing, Stonewall's a jumpin'-off-place for bounty hunters. And with up to two thousand dollars on Wilkes's head, dependin' on how you want to look at it, about every man in the Nations is a bounty hunter." He shrugged, vaguely surprised at the bullheaded stand he was taking. "Stonewall's out. And every other town. Maybe over in the Choctaw Nation I can get in with a Katy Railroad agent and get him to telegraph a message to the nearest marshal——"

Amilia Rathmore came ramrod-erect on the wagon seat. "The Katy Railroad! That must be fifty miles from here?"

"Closer to eighty. And there's no guarantee it'll do any good when I get there. If I get there."

"I hope," Amilia Rathmore said coldly, "you don't expect me to drive all the way to some railroad town, with a dangerous prisoner in my wagon."

For a moment Kiowa pondered the flightiness of women. "I guess I don't expect anything. I was just tellin' you the way it is. If I have to, I can cut travois poles and drag the hunky behind one of the horses."

"With a broken leg?" Now she was indignant. "It would kill him."

"Not Skoda." Once more Kiowa showed her his mask-like grin. "He's bound he's goin' to cash in on old Judge Parker's hangin' machine in Fort Smith."

"Nevertheless, it would be inhuman subjecting him to the agony of a jolting travois." She hesitated, then dropped the subject and let it lie. "Have you and the prisoners had supper?"

Kiowa said yes, they'd chewed some jerky, and Amilia Rathmore huffed and declared that jerky was all right for staving off starvation for a few days, but nothing to travel or fight on. She snapped the lines over the backs of her team and drove the wagon to the end of the cut-bank, then back down the long grade to where the prisoners were.

"This won't do," she said sharply to Kiowa. "I won't cook a meal this close to dead animals."

"It don't matter," he told her. "We can't build a fire anyway, with the prairie crawlin' with scalp hunters."

She pushed her sunbonnet back and peered at him through the thick lenses of her spectacles. "Don't talk foolishness, Mr. Jones. You'll never make it to the railroad, much less Fort Smith, chewing on dry jerky." She whipped the lines around the brake handle and had climbed over the wagon wheel before it occurred to Kiowa to help her down. "You can let the tail gate down, Mr. Jones. When you've finished with that, you can help me get Mr. Skoda into the wagon."

Kiowa blinked at her, trying to determine if she was serious. He came to the gloomy conclusion that Amilia Rathmore was always serious. Humourless, hardheaded, impulsive, reckless, not to mention homely—a dangerous and uncomfortable combination, any way you looked at it. But she had a wagon, a sound team and a load of supplies, all of which Kiowa needed badly. So he swallowed his objections, let down the tail gate and wrestled the hunky into the wagon.

"You could be right about moving away from this cut-bank," he had to admit. "Somebody besides you might have heard the shootin'."

"There's a creek over to the east of here," she told him, going her own feminine, single-track way. "Plenty of water and wood, a good place to make camp and cook supper."

"Look here, Miss Rathmore, I told you . . ."

He might as well have been talking to the wind. She merely peered at him with her magnified eyes and shook her head pityingly. "There's nothing to worry about, Mr. Jones. Not for the present, at least. Even if someone saw our fire and came to investigate, what would they see? A woman and her husband camping on the trail—there's nothing unusual or suspicious about a family travelling through the Nations."

Kiowa held his head and groaned. All of a sudden they were a family—man and wife! He wondered how she meant to explain the prisoners.

"I understand," she told him soberly, "that this has been a difficult day for you. But you're to be commended for taking the prisoners in hand, and fighting off those bounty hunters. You've no reason to be downhearted."

Kiowa opened his mouth but the words stuck in his throat. No reason to be downhearted! He had killed two men and saddled himself with two murderers and a woman school-teacher who could shoot like a mountain man but didn't have the common sense of a snubbing post. Within the last two days his life had been turned inside out, and for all he knew the whole pack, himself included, might come down with smallpox before the night was over. But according to Amilia Rathmore, everything was fine!

He had the good sense to walk off while he was still too aggravated to speak, willing to put up with almost anything for the chance of getting his prisoners to some railroad town and set himself free of the responsibility.

Levi Skoda, wedged in between sacks of flour and feather bedding, called to Kiowa from the back of the wagon. "Jones, you've got no right to drag Miss Rathmore into this thing."

"What would you want to do?" Kiowa almost snarled. "Ride a travois to Fort Smith?"

"Yes," the hunky said without hesitation. "She's a good woman. You ought not get her mixed up with the likes of us."

Kiowa said wryly, "I'll tell you somethin', Skoda. Don't worry about Miss Rathmore. She can take care of herself."

He moved on to Bobby Jack and unlocked his leg irons. "What's this all about?" the assassin demanded.

"We're movin'. Get on your feet."

Bobby Jack shot him a narrow look. "Travellin'? To-night?"

Amilia Rathmore called from the wagon seat. "Please move along, Mr. Jones. We've a way to go, you know, and the moon won't stay bright all night."

Bobby Jack gaped. Then he snorted, threw his head back and laughed in Kiowa's angry face.

They made camp that night beside a nameless stream that meandered down, clear and cold, from the higher country to the east, from the Kiamichis and the Ozarks. Amilia Rathmore built her fire and fried dry-salt pork and spuds and onions, and topped it off with fresh-pounded coffee and corn-dodgers. It had been a long time since Kiowa had eaten as well, and he had to admit, grudgingly, that their situation looked less bleak with a belly full of hot grub.

But the fire made him nervous, and he kicked it out as soon as the meal was cooked. He saw that Bobby Jack's leg irons were tight, then handcuffed him to a wagon wheel for the night. The assassin, full of good food and coffee, had regained his normal pose of sneering superiority.

"You look worried, cowboy. And you ought to. Them scalp hunters to-day, they're just the beginnin'. You know that, don't you?"

"There was a time, not far back," Kiowa told him, "when I was all for turnin' you loose just to keep from lookin' at you. But the more you talk the more I side with that government marshal that was so dead set on gettin' you to a federal courtroom."

Bobby Jack grinned in his irritating way. "The marshal couldn't do it. What makes you think you can do it, Jones?"

Kiowa shrugged. "I don't aim to try. But with a little luck I can get you to a railroad town and send for another marshal."

The young assassin snorted. "Luck don't come in that big a package. You'll be dead before this time to-morrow, cowhand. And I'll be free."

Kiowa wheeled stiffly and tramped to the edge of the clearing to tend to the horse that had belonged to the bounty hunter Morgan. One thing about Morgan, he'd had a good eye for horseflesh. This one was a close-coupled little bay, not quite fifteen hands but broad and deep-shouldered and as powerful as a buffalo. A proud, fox-eared aristocratic stallion, everything a fine quarter horse ought to be but seldom was. This one must have cost Morgan a pretty penny—assuming, of course, that the bounty hunter hadn't stolen him.

Kiowa watered the stallion, along with the team and the second saddle animal, the grey gelding that had belonged to the young bushwhacker called Jelly. Then he fed the stallion a handful of shelled corn out of the dead marshal's pack rig and staked all animals nearby where they would be handy. When he came back to camp Miss Amilia Rathmore was sitting on the wagon tongue.

"Hadn't you better turn in, Miss Rathmore? To-morrow's apt to be a long day."

He moved closer, not seeing too well in the moonlight, but well enough to make out that there was a considerable change in the way Amilia Rathmore looked. Something about her hair was different; it was softer, not pulled back so severely as it had been before. But the thing that made the big difference was that she had shucked her spectacles. Her eyes, no longer distorted and magnified by the thick lenses, found their proper place in her face. And her face, if not beautiful, was at least less homely than before.

One thing that hadn't changed was her snippishness. "What," she demanded, "are you staring at, Mr. Jones?"

Kiowa shuffled in vague discomfort. "You, I guess; what'd you do to yourself? You lose your specs?"

She studied him silently for several seconds. "Is there any reason," she asked coolly, "why I shouldn't wear or not wear my spectacles, as I see fit?"

"Well, no, ma'am, I guess not. . . ." He shuffled again, scratching his bristling chin. "I mean, sure, it's all right with me, if you don't want to wear 'em. I just figured maybe you needed them to see with."

Amilia Rathmore quickly looked away, her face burning, shamed. Kiowa, in his blunt way, had driven straight to the truth. She was vain, though only heaven knew why, considering that she was thirty-two years old, in a country where women past twenty were, as a matter of course, branded "old maid." True, she was practically blind without her spectacles, which, as a rule, she removed only for sleeping. She knew what she looked like, and she knew how the thick lenses made something grotesque of her eyes and face, but this streak of vanity had showed itself unexpectedly, surprising her even more than it had Kiowa.

She fumbled in the slash pocket of her skirts for the spectacles, but her hands—the same hands that had been so steady when fighting off the bounty hunters—were suddenly all thumbs.

Kiowa frowned, puzzled at the woman's actions, then spoke with profound ignorance. "Somethin' the matter, Miss Rathmore? You look a mite flustered."

She made a small sound, a strange sound for such a woman, and lurched up from the wagon tongue. ". . . Good night, Mr. Jones."

Kiowa shrugged. He had never pretended to understand the flightiness of women, and he didn't mean to commence it now. "Good night, Miss Rathmore I'll throw my roll over by the live oak, in case you need me."

"I won't need you, or anybody else, Mr. Jones," she blurted.

Kiowa blinked, then shrugged again and walked away.

Sleeping with one eye open, his thoughts drifting in a kind of half-consciousness that he had mastered on a thousand night watches, Kiowa dimly pondered the phenomenon who called herself Amilia Rathmore. True, the schoolteacher was no beauty out of *Leslie's* or *Harper's Weekly*, not to mention *The Police Gazette*, with or without spectacles; nevertheless, the vision of that plain, straightforward face had somehow stuck in Kiowa's mind. Maybe he'd been riding mills and fences too long. Maybe his system wasn't up to the shock of being suddenly thrown in with a decent woman after all these months of talking to a bunch of breachy range cows and a few hammerheaded horses. It was a well-known fact that a decent woman was the most dangerous thing there was, unless maybe it was a night stampede in cut-bank country. Dance-hall girls were something else—after the cuts and bruises healed you could put them out of your mind. But decent women, or "good women," as they were known in the range country, had always been a puzzle to Kiowa. They said one thing and meant another, which could get a man in a mess of trouble, and sometimes even married.

That thought jarred Kiowa to full wakefulness. He shuddered, remembering some of his old bunkhouse cronies who had got themselves trapped in just such a way. Talking when they should have been travelling. Good, hard-bottomed cowhands, one minute as free as a breeze on the Staked Plains, the next minute roped and dragged to the branding fire, shackled to a steady job, as surely as Bobby Jack Wilkes was shackled to the wagon wheel.

It was enough to break a man out in cold sweats. Kiowa threw off the tarp cover, sat up and began to build a smoke. Not a simple feat, the way his hands were shaking.

: : : :

Amilia Rathmore had rearranged the wagon load, piling personal belongings and camp supplies at either end of the wagon box, creating a kind of cumbersome privacy, and protection—if it should come to that. Levi Skoda had been moved out of the wagon and on to the ground with Bobby Jack for the night.

Miss Rathmore was also having trouble sleeping. Not that she was afraid, or had ever been afraid, of the ordinary run of dangers. Her father had been a circuit-riding preacher in Comanche country when it had been worth a person's scalp to venture unarmed more than a few hundred yards from the family sod hut. But this was no common run of danger. It was nothing that she could aim a rifle at. This time the danger was within herself. A recklessness, born of desperation too long suppressed. And it was a strange and frightening thing, after all these years of shifting for herself, cherishing her independence, or telling herself that she did.

Something had happened to-night that cracked the shell of her smugness; something that she would be a long time forgetting, and maybe she never would forget it. To-night she had made a fool of herself, making up to a man, frizzing her hair like any trail-town doxy, trying to go without her spectacles. But the most humiliating thing of all was in her choice of men. She could easily imagine a woman, any woman, becoming slightly giddy if she should suddenly find herself thrown in with a presentable, cultured, considerate gentleman, perhaps a professional man, a lawyer or doctor, even a clergyman. But not the likes of Kiowa Jones! A gangly, hatchet-faced, grub-line rider, who, in all probability, had never earned as much as thirty dollars in any single month of his life. A drifter, a carouser (no doubt), a slovenly saddle tramp totally lacking in ambition, education, and any trace of finesse. Possibly he was competent at working cattle, but he was almost criminally inept with firearms, and in a country where some skill with guns might well mean the difference between living and dying.

Not a pretty or pleasant picture, but a reasonably accurate picture of Kiowa Jones as Amilia Rathmore saw him. And yet she had thrown herself at him, or would have if he had been less crude, less blunt, less infuriatingly honest—if he had given her the slightest chance. Which he hadn't.

She lay rigidly on her wagon-box pallet, staring unblinkingly at the dirty grey wagon sheet sagging on the bows over her head, wanting to cry her shame but hardheadedly denying herself that small comfort.

A twig snapped in the night not far from the wagon. Someone was out there, skulking about the camp. Instead of being frightened, as most women would, Amilia Rathmore welcomed any threat, any danger that might be countered with a gun.

The change was remarkable. Suddenly she was the Amilia Rathmore of the cut-bank fight, moving swiftly, with full confidence in her own abilities and judgment. She grabbed the well-used Winchester and thrust it through the puckered opening in the wagon sheet.

"I see you! Don't move!"

Several tense seconds passed. Finally, Amilia Rathmore said in an entirely different voice, one that she couldn't recognize as her own: "Oh, it's you, Mr. Jones. . . ."

Kiowa swallowed, eyeing the rifle nervously. "Just checkin' around the camp, Miss Rathmore. Didn't aim to wake you up."

"Is anything wrong?"

"Everything's fine, Miss Rathmore," he said with just a trace of gall. "Well, I guess I'll be turnin' in."

"Mr. Jones . . ."

Kiowa hesitated, looking back at the wagon.

After a short pause, Amilia Rathmore said stiffly, "Good night, Mr. Jones." And a drop curtain fell over the opening.

CHAPTER SIX

TO KIOWA'S SURPRISE, the night passed peacefully. At first light he rounded up the horses and Amilia Rathmore started breakfast. Bobby Jack Wilkes was awake and complaining about the service.

"Look here, Jones, these wrist irons're too tight. You want to shut off circulation and start gangrene? Is that what you're after?"

Kiowa ignored him and looked at Skoda's leg. It was puffy and discoloured beneath the splints, but that was to be expected. "How you feel, Levi?"

The little hunky nodded.

"It won't be much fun in that wagon to-day. We've got some creeks to cross before we get to the sandstone country, and that won't be much better."

"Thanks anyhow," Skoda said huskily, "but there's no need to worry about me, Jones. I'll make it to Fort Smith. You couldn't keep me from it, even if you wanted to."

Bobby Jack snorted. "I'm startin' to get a little tired of that hoodoo talk, hunky."

Skoda shrugged, closed his eyes and shut out the world of reality, Bobby Jack and all. Kiowa went over to the fire where Amilia Rathmore was turning spuds in an iron skillet. "How is Mr. Skoda's leg?" she asked without looking up from her work.

"Swole some, but I don't think he feels it. He's a queer one, that hunky."

"Why do you call him that? I thought he was a gipsy."

Kiowa hunkered by the fire and built a cigarette. "I guess he is—some kind of a breed gipsy, anyhow. See that scar on his ear? That's where he used to wear a ring, if I'm any judge. His wife was gipsy, the one he murdered."

Miss Rathmore shot him a look of distaste, but Kiowa didn't see it, wouldn't have recognized it if he had seen it. "Stabbed her with a skinnin' knife," he went on conversationally. "Maybe he had his reasons. I guess he did. That's how it goes, maybe, when a man's stuck with one woman all the time. Sooner or later he gets his fill of it and"—he slashed the air, indicating a knife cut—"and that's all there is to it."

She raised her head and fixed him with another look, this one so dark and pointed that it could not be mistaken or ignored. Kiowa decided it was time to make his roll, tie it and stow it in the back of the wagon. But in a little while he was back at the fire. "Gipsies, in a lot of ways, are like Indians," he said, picking up the conversation as though nothing had happened. "I guess they had a place once, some country that belonged just to them, but not any more, so they say. So they figure it's the gipsies against the world. Like the Indians. And they band together and do the best they can, thievin', fightin', schemin' at different ways of getting at the rest of us, before we get at them. A hardheaded bunch. They got their own chiefs and medicine men, like the Indians. There's not a place in the country that wants them, or ain't a little bit scared of them, or a little bit shamed because everybody treats them the way they do. Like the Indians."

Amilia straightened slowly from the cooking fire and looked at this homely, bearded cowhand almost as though she had never seen him before. "I didn't realize that you knew so much about gipsies."

"I don't. But I know Indians. Now and again gipsy bands—caravans, they call them—used to pass through trail towns up in Kansas, the women tellin' fortunes and stealin', the men swappin' horses and stealin', the kids just stealin'. I was fresh off the reservation where I was raised, and they took me for a young Kiowa that had come up north to see the elephant, as the sayin' goes. I was the only cowhand in town that didn't get robbed half-blind."

Kiowa grinned to himself, remembering. Hunkering beside the fire, idly poking at the coals with a stick, he could almost forget that this was a woman he was talking to, and a schoolteacher to boot. The talk came naturally, as unaffected and free-flowing as the cow talk of roundup hands after a day's gather.

"A caravan passed through Tascosa once when I was there," he rambled on. "Wagons painted all colours, the horses all duded up with jinglebobs and bells and ribbons in their tails and manes, the women rigged out like for a Mex fiesta, the men with that look in their eyes that said, 'Go easy, gents. It's cold steel for supper to the first man to look slantwise at our women.' When they left Tascosa, most of the chickens, a goat, a milk cow, two pigs and some dogs went with them." Kiowa laughed. "Like the Indians. They don't steal to live. With them it's the sport of the thing."

Miss Rathmore removed her spectacles for wiping, and the figure of Kiowa Jones became blurred and softened, and for a moment he was something more than a scrubby, unlettered fence rider. For just an instant she was on the verge of understanding what it was about him that had caused her to make a fool of herself. Then Bobby Jack Wilkes yelled:

"Jones, you aim to gab all day, or do you aim to feed us?"

Amilia Rathmore replaced her spectacles, and the moment of revelation vanished like smoke talk in a plains wind.

They forded the Middle Boggy that morning and headed north, giving Stonewall a wide berth. That afternoon they raised the sandy, almost bankless Canadian, and inched along the scrub-timber country of the bottom, heading generally to the east, toward the Choctaw Nation. It was heavy going for the wagon, hard on the team and even harder on the white-faced hunky in the back of the wagon.

Amilia Rathmore gestured from the wagon seat. "Mr. Jones, I understand that following an established road or trail might be unwise, but isn't there a less difficult route we might take?"

Kiowa kneed his sturdy bay alongside the wagon. "If there's an easier way, I don't know about it. But we'll be hard to spot here in the brush; I wouldn't like our chances out there on the prairie."

"Do you believe there might actually be more bounty hunters looking for Mr. Wilkes?"

Kiowa merely grinned wryly and built a cigarette. Fishing in his hatband for a match, he said, "We ain't runnin' on any hard and fast schedule. When you want to take a breather, give a holler."

He eased back to the rear of the wagon and looked in on Skoda. In answer to the usual questions, Levi nodded or shook his head, afraid to trust his voice. Bobby Jack, handcuffed and tied to his saddle, trailed the wagon at the end of a lead rope. With a quiet intensity, he was watching two horsemen who had just appeared on a grassy rise overlooking the river.

"You see that, Jones?" He shot Kiowa a coyote grin, indicating the riders with a jerk of his head.

"Indians," Kiowa said, with more hope than confidence.

"They don't look like Indians to me, cowboy."

Kiowa looked again, but they were too far away to make out any details. "Indians," he said again. "Chickasaws look like anybody else at that distance."

But Bobby Jack heard the note of concern and his grin widened. Kiowa urged the bay forward again and directed Amilia Rathmore to head the wagon into heavier brush.

After an hour Kiowa rode a wide circle around the wagon's position. There was no sign of the horsemen. The sun was beginning to set and wild turkeys were making for their roosting places in the bottom. Several rabbits, out for the late afternoon, darted across Kiowa's trail, and a lithe young doe appeared suddenly almost within pistol range, then sprinted for the brush, white tail bobbing.

A family of Wichitas marched in line formation across the prairie, casting long picket shadows on the bright grass, heading home, most likely, from a visit with friends or relatives up north. But not a sign of the two horsemen.

Kiowa slanted back toward the river, frowning when he saw that Amilia Rathmore had halted the march and apparently was preparing to make camp. " Anything wrong?" he asked. " We've got nearly another hour of travellin' time. . . ."

Then he saw the tensed-up sign of warning in her face. Kiowa shot a glance at Bobby Jack and noted that he had regained his air of cocky superiority. A steely finger raked up Kiowa's back. Cautiously, he climbed down from the saddle, reached for his sheathed Winchester . . .

" Leave it be, cowboy."

A stocky barrel of a man stepped out from behind the wagon, an old-fashioned Prescott revolver aimed squarely at the centre of Kiowa's chest. Kiowa shot another anxious look at Amilia Rathmore.. " You all right? He didn't bother you, did he?"

She smiled weakly. " No. I'm fine. I think it's Mr. Wilkes he's most interested in."

" I figured," Kiowa said wearily. He grounded the bay's reins and studied the man behind the .36 calibre Prescott. One thing was sure, no professional bounty hunter would be carrying a weapon like that old Civil War revolver. Anyhow, the man didn't look like a gunman. Hard fat rolled over the belt of his waist overalls and over the collar of his hickory shirt, and there was the sweaty, faded look of the sodbuster about him. Not that that meant anything. A sodbuster would go after two thousand dollars as fast as a professional scalp hunter.

" There was two of you," Kiowa said, " when I saw you watchin' us from the rise. Where's your partner?"

" Over here, cowboy, with a shotgun aimed at your lady friend's head. In case you get a notion to be a hero."

The voice came from a live oak tree with a tangle of possum grapevines climbing up its trunk. Kiowa turned, but not too suddenly, and the fat man called, " Come on out, Jessie, we got 'em all together now. One of us can loose herd 'em while the other rides after Pa."

A younger, thinner copy of the fat man stepped out from behind the live oak and came forward, grinning widely. " Well, now! Pa'll be right proud of us when he sees how good we done. Won't he, Vitto?" He held a long, choke-barrel shotgun carelessly at Amilia Rathmore's back, but his eyes, angrier than his voice, kept darting in Bobby Jack's direction. "That's him, ain't it, Vitto?" Indicating the assassin with a nod.

"It's him," the fat man said flatly. Then, to Kiowa, "Drop the gunbelt, cowboy."

The voice left no margin for argument. Kiowa slipped the buckle and let the cartridge belt and revolver drop.

"Kick the pistol over here."

Kiowa gave it a kick. The young man, Jessie, grinned. Vitto's expression didn't change.

"Look here," Kiowa heard himself saying, "I'm actin' for a federal marshal. You boys got any notion what it costs to tamper with a government prisoner?"

Vitto gave him a grudging, humourless grin. "We know, mister. And we don't care. The name's Montford; I'm Vitto, that's my kid brother Jessie. I used to have another brother, Bucky, but we had to bury Bucky. So we just don't care."

Kiowa still didn't understand, still thought they were bounty hunters looking to set Wilkes free and collect the two thousand. But Bobby Jack understood, or was beginning to. He was beginning to read the truth in Jessie Montford's eyes, and the slow panic that gradually drained the colour from the assassin's face was not a pleasant thing to see. Amilia Rathmore, in her woman's way, knew instinctively that these two men were after more than bounty. In the back of the wagon, Levi Skoda, although he couldn't see what was going on, could guess what was in the minds of the two brothers. But Kiowa Jones, like a bull pup with its fur roughed up, hated to turn loose of an idea once he'd got his teeth in it.

"You boys work it over in your heads," he said with fake heartiness. "What's a thousand, or even two thousand dollars to do for you, if you go and get the U.S. Marshals on your trail?"

The fat Vitto eyed him silently, then said patiently, "The name Montford don't mean anything to you, does it, friend? Well, it's no great surprise. We're from down east Texas way. Farmers—sodbusters, you'd call us—all but Bucky. He took to workin' cattle. Fiddle-footed, liked to travel. Last we heard from him he was ridin' for an outfit over in the Panhandle, the Rafter-A. . . ."

Kiowa knew the brand, had heard of it, anyway. The Rafter-A, they said, had got into trouble with the Association—the Association being one of those wildcat rules-making outfits that a few range-grabbing cowmen like to organize for the purpose of riding herd on outsiders. The Rafter-A, so the story had it, was an outsider that wouldn't be herded. Just the kind of situation that kept professional murderers like Bobby Jack Wilkes in business.

Now, at last, Kiowa was beginning to get it. Shooting a slitted glance at the Montfords, he said, in a voice so cool and unruffled that it surprised him, "You boys aim to take over the law business and save the courts some time and trouble . . . is that it?"

Vitto Montford shrugged. "That's about it."

Jessie Montford laughed, gazing steadily at the young assassin. "We come a long way, mister, to see you swing."

"Ride a little farther, to Fort Smith," Kiowa argued, "and see it done right."

Vitto shook his head, his fat neck bulging. "Pa won't hear of it. We got to do it ourselves."

"Even if it gets you hung yourselves?"

"No matter what," Vitto said heavily, with a trace of weariness, even reluctance. "This is the way it's got to be. We don't like to beat you out of your bounty money, but—"

Kiowa, snarling in quick anger: "I didn't get in this thing for the bounty!"

Vitto grunted, not caring one way or another. Then, speaking over his shoulder to his younger brother: "Get me some piggin' string, Jessie. Looks like we better tie the cowhand up for a spell."

Angrily, Kiowa was about to tell them they couldn't get away with what they were doing, then realized how ridiculous it would sound. They were doing it. And with very little effort.

"What about the woman?" Jessie asked.

"Just the cowhand. I don't reckon a woman can ramble

far in this brush." Vitto smiled feebly in Amilia Rathmore's direction. "You much of a hand with a skillet, ma'am? Me and Jessie, we ain't et in two days, except for some Comanche pemmican."

Miss Rathmore drew herself up haughtily, but Kiowa caught her attention and nodded. Grudgingly, she agreed to break out her cooking utensils while Jessie rustled wood for a fire. For the present they let Bobby Jack stay where he was, astride his horse, handcuffed to the saddle horn. Kiowa was made to sit on the ground beside the wagon while Vitto tied his hands and feet with whang strings.

The two brothers ate heartily and silently of fried dry-salt meat, home-canned tomatoes and hoecake.

Jessie sopped the last of his tomato juice out of Miss Rathmore's bone china dinner plate. "You aim to fetch Pa, Vitto, or you want me to do it?"

Vitto studied his prisoners. "You're lighter and can ride faster. I aim to get this over with just as fast as we can."

The younger brother grunted, wiped his mouth with the back of his hand and turned his shotgun over to Vitto. "I'll have Pa here in time for breakfast." He touched his hatbrim to Amilia Rathmore. "Tasty vittles, ma'am. I'm obliged." He turned and headed for the brush where he had tied up. In a few minutes they heard him leaving the river bottom at an easy lope, glimpsed him once or twice through the scrub oaks and cottonwoods, and then he was gone.

Vitto Montford sighed, took the shotgun and spoke to Kiowa. "You got the key to the prisoner's irons?"

Kiowa nodded. "In my pocket."

Vitto got the key, released Bobby Jack and pulled him down from the saddle. "Listen to me!" the assassin blurted. "I can make you a rich man, Montford. I've got money, plenty of it, in half the banks in Texas, and some in Kansas besides. I'll give it to you, more money than you can count. All you've got to do is let me go. . . ."

In a cold, offhanded way, Vitto struck the young assassin a tremendous blow. Bobby Jack reeled back against the wagon, his mouth bloody, his cheek split on the inside, "Any way you take it," the fat man told him, "you'll be swingin' from a cottonwood come first light. You can live out the night in peace, or I can truss you up and stuff your mouth with your bandanna. It's up to you."

If looks could kill, Vitto Montford would have been ready for burying. Spewing blood, Bobby Jack wiped the back of his cuffed hand across his mouth. But all he said was, "All right, mister. It's your play."

Vitto sat him down, put the irons on his legs and chained him to the wagon wheel. Amilia Rathmore, saying nothing, showing nothing by way of action or expression, cooked another skillet of dry-salt and fed Kiowa and Skoda. The fat man paid almost no attention to the lame hunky.

"We've got a little wait," he told Miss Rathmore. "I don't favour bindin' up a woman, if it can be helped. You give your word to behave, ma'am?"

"Miss," she corrected automatically. Then, nodding, "You have my word."

"Pull up the cowhand's roll and keep the fire goin'." Vitto took his shotgun about twenty paces from the fire and settled for the night's watch. For a while the bloody afterglow of the sun painted the western horizon, then night came down and lay softly on the prairie.

Amilia Rathmore built up the fire, slanting a questioning glance in Kiowa's direction. Kiowa pretended not to see it. She was, in her silent way, asking him to indicate what she must do, and Kiowa didn't know. Bound hand and foot, he was as helpless as Bobby Jack or Levi Skoda. There was nothing that he or Miss Rathmore could do against Vitto's shotgun.

For a while the only sound was the crackling of the fire and Skoda's restless shifting inside the wagon. Then the hunky called, "Miss Rathmore, you reckon I could have a drink of water?"

Amilia turned to look at Vitto Montford, and the fat man nodded. "All right, but no tricks." He got up and followed Miss Rathmore, his eyes missing nothing as she took the wagon canteen off its peg and handed it to Levi.

" He's feverish," she said, placing the back of her hand to Skoda's forehead. " I'll leave the canteen with him. If you have no objections, Mr. Montford."

Vitto shrugged, followed her back to the fire, then took up his original position where he could cover the whole wagon area with the shotgun.

" This here's a hammerheaded play," Kiowa said wearily. " Wilkes is goin' to get hisself hung pretty soon, it don't matter what you Montfords do about it. You reckon it's goin' to be worth your own neck, and your brother's, and your pa's, just to hurry the hangin' by a few days, or weeks?"

Vitto shifted heavily, peered at Kiowa and said nothing.

" It's bad medicine, Vitto, lynchin' a government prisoner."

" It's worse medicine murderin' a Montford," he said flatly, looking at Bobby Jack Wilkes.

" Stringin' up this killer—you reckon that's goin' to bring your brother back?"

Vitto, after a taut silence, said, " You talk too goddamn much."

Kiowa leaned back against the wagon wheel. Then he came suddenly erect, startled, as a dribble of cold water struck his left shoulder.

" What's the matter with you now?" Vitto demanded, beginning to lose his patience.

Kiowa scowled, tried to shrug. " This ain't exactly the most comfortable way to spend a night." But he shook his head, quickly, when Vitto grudgingly offered to have a look at the whang strings on his wrists. Those few drops of water—he wanted to know where they had come from, and why.

Another drop fell lightly to the brim of Kiowa's hat. Above him, in the wagon box, he could hear the hunky stirring, and Kiowa began to understand what was happening. He looked quickly at Amilia Rathmore, but her face told nothing. Kiowa hunched his shoulders and scooted a little to the left. A thin liquid stream dripped down from a crack in the wagon box, wetting the sleeve of his canvas jacket. He experimented in moving his bound hands from one side to the other, until at last he felt a few drops of water fall on his wrists. That was the place. He held that position rigidly until the whang leather was thoroughly soaked. In a little while the trickle stopped. Skoda's canteen had gone empty.

Kiowa worked slowly, carefully, at stretching the whang strings. The tough leather strips became slick and rubbery and finally began to give. He sat very still for several minutes, giving his breathing a chance to catch its normal rhythm.

"I got a cramp in my shoulder," he complained to Vitto. "How about tyin' my hands in front for a spell?"

The fat man scowled, then got to his feet, cradling the shotgun in the crook of his left arm. He tramped toward the wagon to have a closer look. "You don't look in such a bad way," he said suspiciously.

"It's my shoulder," Kiowa told him.

The fat man made a weary, grunting sound. Using great caution, Kiowa slipped his hands out of the slippery leather. "Scoot around," Vitto told him, "and I'll tie you up in front."

Montford rested the shotgun against the wagon wheel. Kiowa lurched to his knees and lashed out with all the strength he could call up. Kiowa's fist sank almost wrist-deep into the hard fat above Vitto's gut. The fat man blinked, surprised but not hurt. He sized the situation up in an instant and grabbed for the shotgun, but Kiowa had already thought of that and had his hands on the stock.

Vitto grunted, mildly irritated but not greatly concerned. He took a quick dancing step backward, then kicked viciously with a heavy boot and the shotgun went flying out of Kiowa's hand. Kiowa, forgetting for the moment that his feet were still tied, tried to pull himself upright and fell on his face.

Vitto grinned dangerously. "That was a mistake, cowboy. Yes, sir, a real bad mistake." He jerked the ancient Prescott .36 out of his waistband and started a wide, skull-cracking swing, aimed at the back of Kiowa's head.

But Vitto had made a mistake himself, turning his back to Amilia Rathmore. She darted for the shotgun, grasping the thin part of the stock with both hands, and swung the heavy barrel at Vitto's head. The fat man's limp-brim hat flew off, a rush of blood welling up over his right ear. Vitto stumbled in mid-swing and fell heavily against the wagon box. For an instant his eyes shone glassily in the firelight as he stared, amazed, at Amilia Rathmore. Slowly he melted to the ground, a mound of fat, silent, still.

Bobby Jack Wilkes let out a yell of laughter. "You get a look at his eyes, ma'am, just before he keeled over? Wasn't that the damnedest sight you ever saw?"

Miss Rathmore wheeled on the assassin, still holding the shotgun as if it were a club. "That's enough of your hard talk, Mr. Wilkes."

Bobby Jack gave her a long, careful look. "Whatever you say . . . miss."

Amilia drew a skinning knife from Vitto's belt sheath and cut the strings that bound Kiowa's feet. Kiowa felt his own head, as though it surprised him to find it in one piece, then he looked in wonder at Amilia Rathmore. "That's the second time you've stepped in and saved my hide," he said in an accusing voice.

Amilia Rathmore flushed but held her temper. "Mr. Montford will be coming to soon. Hadn't you better . . .?"

Kiowa got himself to his feet. "There's another set of irons in my saddlebags. That was your big mistake," he said to the mound of tallow. "If you'd used shackles instead of whang leather you wouldn't be in the fix you're in." He looked in at the back of the wagon and grinned wanly at the little hunky. "Thanks, Levi. I don't know if it'll help you, but if we ever see a U.S. Marshal I'll tell him how you helped stall off a lynchin'."

Skoda shook his head. "It wasn't for you, Jones. And it wasn't for that money killer down there. It was for Miss Rathmore."

"You hear that, Miss Rathmore?" Bobby Jack grinned. "The hunky's startin' to make up to you. Another day or so maybe he'll even offer to marry you, if you can keep him off old Judge Parker's hangin' machine."

Amilia Rathmore's eyes flashed behind her thick lenses. Kiowa came forward with a curiously rigid stride and started unlocking the assassin's irons.

"What you doin'?" Bobby Jack demanded worriedly.

"Takin' the chains off, just long enough to teach you some manners." But Miss Rathmore took his arm and held it firmly. "It doesn't matter, Mr. Jones. Nothing his kind says could ever matter to decent people." She nodded at Vitto Montford, who was beginning to stir. "Don't you think you ought to see about the irons?"

Kiowa cooled down enough to relock Wilkes's handcuffs, then went after the irons for Vitto.

Rage crowded the fat man's eyes when he saw the chains on his hands and feet, and Kiowa knew exactly, to the word, what he was going to say. "You'll be sorry for this, Jones!"

Kiowa had a hysterical urge to laugh, but his face was frozen. He got some cleaning patches and gun oil from his saddlebag, walked off a piece where he could keep an eye on the wagon, and went to work on his much-abused revolver and Winchester. Amilia Rathmore came over to the cottonwood log where he was sitting.

"You better get some sleep," Kiowa told her.

Miss Rathmore smiled weakly. "Don't expect me to sleep, Mr. Jones. Not to-night. Not until that other Montford boy comes with his father and this misunderstanding is settled."

Kiowa peered at her through slitted eyes. "Misunderstanding," he said, the word puckering his mouth like a green persimmon. "When they get here, that Montford boy, as you call him, and his old man will likely try to kill the bunch of us. They'll *have* to, if they get their hands on Wilkes and hang him. I don't think old man Montford will be the kind to leave witnesses behind to testify against him in a federal court."

Amilia Rathmore's eyes grew large behind the thick glass of her spectacles. "What do you intend to do?"

"We wait." He worked an oiled patch through the barrel of the saddle gun. "When there's nothin' to do, that's what you do—nothin'." He gestured toward the log. "If you don't aim to sleep, you might as well sit."

They sat in silence for several minutes, Kiowa aware that she was watching him from the corner of her eye. "Do you think we can win over the Montfords, Mr. Jones?"

"Well, we got Vitto. Maybe we can get the old man to trade off, Vitto's life for Wilkes's." But he didn't believe it, and neither did she.

Suddenly she looked tired. It had been a hard, long day, and it was beginning to tell on all of them. "I wish this were over," she said unexpectedly. "I wish I were in Tahlequah. I wish I had my school and my girls. . . ." She looked up, smiled faintly. "I've never seen them, of course, but I think of them as my girls. That's how it is with maiden ladies, Mr. Jones. We pretend."

Kiowa yawned and scratched himself. "Sure, I guess all of us do. When you're out ridin' the fringes, livin' by yourself all winter in some line shack, with nothin' but grey-backs and centipedes for company, why you'd be surprised what goes on inside a lonesome cowhand's head."

She studied him carefully as he worked on his guns, trying to see if he was making cruel fun of her, the way some men did, the way some men figured they had a right and maybe even an obligation to do, with an old maid. But she could hear no snicker behind his words, could see no barbs in the glance he threw at her. He was merely talking to her man to man, the way he might talk to a bunkhouse mate, to kill time—and in a way that was the cruellest cut of all.

Kiowa put the rifle away and started on the revolver. "Anything the matter?" he asked.

"No." Cautiously. "Why?"

"You're quiet all of a sudden."

She hadn't realized that a silence had lain so long between them. "Do you enjoy the work you do, Mr. Jones? Working with cattle, I mean. Other people's cattle. It's a hard, lonesome life, isn't it? There isn't much pay, or chance of advancement."

Now it was his turn to look for barbs. "Sure it's hard," he said defensively, "and lonesome too, sometimes. And I guess a cowhand won't never die from too much rich grub and high livin'. But a top hand can draw his pay any time he feels like it and never have to worry about findin' another job."

She smiled. "So can schoolteachers. Or bank clerks, or blacksmiths."

Kiowa blinked. For some reason he had always believed that self-sufficiency was limited exclusively to men who worked with cattle. "Well," he said, hedging a bit, "a cow-hand, he's got no boss to plague him all the time, he does as he pleases, he's free as the wind out on the high plains." He grinned, figuring he'd nailed the lid shut on that discussion.

"Living all winter by yourself," she said meekly, "in a filthy little dugout, working twelve to eighteen hours a day in all kinds of weather—is that what you call being free and doing as you please?"

Kiowa's neck was beginning to burn. He could handle a stiff rope in the rain, or a green bronc on a cold morning, or even a spooky herd in a thunderstorm, most of the time, but he handled words like a Cheyenne dog soldier struggling with a knife and fork. This conversation, the way it was working out, was going to be uphill the rest of the way, and he'd just as soon skip it. "Maybe," he said with elaborate concern, "I better take another look at the prisoners."

CHAPTER SEVEN

IT WAS EARLY MORNING, dew-wet, black-green, cold. Kiowa had kicked out the fire and the prisoners were complaining.

"It's bad enough bein' chained to a wagon wheel all night," Bobby Jack Wilkes whined, "but you got no call to let us freeze."

"You're no colder'n the rest of us," Kiowa told him.

Vitto Montford sneered. "Pa and Jess don't need a fire to shoot by, cowhand. They ain't in so big a hurry that they can't lay out and wait for the sun."

And Bobby Jack said, "Look here, Jones . . ." The cocky young assassin was clearly scared, his throat drawn so tight that his voice seemed to come off the roof of his mouth. "Look here, Jones, you ain't got a chance of fightin' off the Montfords. You got to let me loose from here, give me a fightin' chance."

"How much fightin' chance did you give my brother, money killer?" Vitto demanded coldly.

"I don't know your brother. I don't know what you're talkin' about."

Kiowa groaned to himself. "Shut up, both of you, or I'll stuff your mouths with your own shirt-tails." He went to the back of the wagon and looked in on Skoda.

"What do your hoodoo cards say about the Montfords, Levi?"

The little hunky grinned faintly and shook his head. "It's not the cards that's hoodooed, Jones. It's us."

"You're the cheerful cuss, ain't you?"

Levi shrugged. "It's what I see in the tarot. The Hangin' Man, the Lightnin'-struck Tower, a thousand Swords. All the bad cards, like there wasn't any other kind. And Death. Every time I lay them out it comes up Death."

"*La Morte,*" Kiowa said acidly.

Levi was looking less and less like Levi Skoda, the frontier gambler, and more and more like Levi Skodaschinski, the gipsy witchman. Or a little dried-up Kiowa medicine man who, feeling the black hawk on his shoulder, turns his face to the sun and starts his chant of the dead. "*La Morte,*" he said, and closed his eyes.

It was the chill, gun-steel part of the morning, the last dark before the light, the time of the last night watch for those lucky enough to be out with a herd. For Kiowa it was a time of approaching trouble. He could hear it coming, but only in his mind.

The morning was silent, quieter than a Caddo scout sneaking up on a band of Comanche horses. Kiowa's stomach was empty, and sour with sleeplessness. He walked off from the wagon, listening to every small sound of the waking day, wondering if the Montfords were already out there somewhere, waiting for daylight, or if they were still on the road. Then he turned and was startled to find Amilia Rathmore at his elbow.

"What in tarnation do you mean, sneakin' up on a man like that?"

"I didn't sneak," she said loftily. "If you didn't hear me

come up from the wagon, it was because your mind was somewhere else."

He realized that she was right, and he wanted to tell her so, but for the life of him he couldn't find the words. "I was thinking," she said, "that if we had some hot coffee . . ."

"No fire." Kiowa was adamant. "I don't aim to give the Montfords any better target than I have to." He spread his hands in a gesture of helplessness. "I ask your pardon, Miss Rathmore. I didn't aim to raise my voice."

She studied him with a slow smile. "That's all right, Mr. Jones. We're all on edge. It's funny, in a way, isn't it . . .?"

Kiowa scowled. "Is it?"

"I mean, the way things have worked out for us. You didn't want the responsibility of seeing these prisoners to Fort Smith, but here you are, getting set to protect them with your life, for the second time within twenty-four hours."

He grinned humourlessly. "What about yourself? You'd be a good piece on your way to Tahlequah, to that school of yours, if you hadn't decided to throw in with this outfit. I guess that's somethin' else I better ask your pardon for."

She peered at him through the thick lenses. "That won't be necessary, Mr. Jones." With a little nod, she turned and went back to the wagon.

: : : :

The two Montfords arrived with the first light, just as Jessie had promised, in time for breakfast. If there had been breakfast.

"Vitto, it's us," the younger brother called. "Everything all right up there?"

Kiowa could hear the horses upstream, in the brush, but he couldn't see them or the riders. With Vitto's shotgun held so that the muzzle almost touched the fat man's forehead, Kiowa said quietly, "Tell 'em to come on in."

"Go to hell," Vitto snarled.

Kiowa cocked the hammer. "Listen to me, mister. I killed two men yesterday. It was a hard thing, I hated it, but I know now that I can do it if I have to. So I'll ask you once more. Tell 'em to come in."

Vitto's face glistened. His eyes darted like the eyes of a wild thing with the hounds after it.

Jessie Montford called the second time. " Vitto, it's us, me and Pa. Can you hear me?"

Vitto cleared his throat. " I hear you."

Another voice, a thinner, more astringent voice, called, " Vitto, you all right?"

" Tell him to shut up the chin music," Kiowa hissed, " and come on in and get it over with."

Vitto, as if he were reading it from a book, repeated Kiowa's words. " Shut up the chin music. Come on in and get it over with."

In the brush there was a moment of silence. Then Jessie came into the open and started up the sandy slope toward the wagon. " Where's the old man?" Kiowa demanded.

" What'd you do with Pa?" Vitto shouted.

Jessie laughed. " He mislaid a box of shells and wouldn't come without he had plenty of ammunition. He'll be up in a minute."

Kiowa motioned for Amilia Rathmore to move toward the rear of the wagon until he got Jessie and the old man covered. Jessie, grinning to himself, whistling softly between his teeth, came on toward the wagon. Kiowa noted that he had a coil of new hemp rope slung over his shoulder and across his chest, like a bandolier on a Mexican *bandido*.

The old man still hadn't come out of the brush.

" Where're you at, Vitto?" Jessie asked.

" Never mind," Kiowa said, sliding into view around the side of the wagon. Jessie broke his stride. The whistling stopped. He looked at Kiowa, then at the Winchester.

" You know, cowboy, I kind of figured somethin' like this might of happened. Vitto, he tends to get a little careless."

" If you figured it," Kiowa said dryly, " then you're a fool to come walkin' into camp unarmed."

Jessie grinned, unruffled, undisturbed, and a familiar warning ripple went up Kiowa's back. " Where's your pa, Jessie?"

The younger Montford brother came on at the same loose-hipped gait. " Kind of look behind you, cowhand. But don't move too sudden. Pa's got the drop on Miss Rathmore, and what with a long ride on an empty gut, he's a mite nervous in the trigger finger."

Kiowa's cocksureness sagged like lead weights in his belly. He half-turned and saw the old man coming out of the brush on the river side of camp, a gaunt, leathery old sodbuster, as grimly solemn as a Cheyenne shaman taking oath for a sun dance.

Jessie laughed under his breath. "You don't know Pa, mister, but them that knows him wouldn't tell him to shut up when he's a mind to talk. And I guess Vitto knows Pa about as well as anybody."

So that was it. Vitto repeating Kiowa's commands word for word had warned the Montfords that something was wrong.

Ott Montford, although he was inches shorter than his sons, seemed to tower over them. He came toward the wagon in that curious walking lope of a plough jockey, glaring at Kiowa and Vitto while keeping a long-barrelled squirrel rifle aimed at Amilia Rathmore. For the moment he ignored Bobby Jack Wilkes, refusing to look in the assassin's direction. There'd be time enough for Bobby Jack. Later.

"Jones?" the old man demanded, looking at Kiowa.

Kiowa cleared his throat and nodded, wondering what chance he'd have of shooting the old man before Ott Montford could put a bullet in Miss Rathmore. He didn't like the odds. At the old man's nod, Kiowa carefully leaned his rifle against the wagon.

Ott Montford said, "Tell your woman to let my boy go."

Without arguing the point of possession, Kiowa glanced at Miss Rathmore and nodded.

Amilia Rathmore bristled. "Listen to me, Mr. Montford. Mr. Jones is acting on orders from a U.S. Deputy Marshal. Mr. Wilkes is a federal prisoner, and you and your sons will have to answer to a federal court . . ."

Ott Montford, in no mood for talk, especially female talk, casually turned his rifle on Kiowa and said, "I give you just as much time as it takes a toad to hop three times, ma'am, then I shoot your man."

Amilia Rathmore paled.

"One hop," the old man said flatly.

Kiowa, not trusting a female to make up her own mind, spoke quickly, "The key's in my shirt pocket."

Jessie grinned. Vitto shot an uneasy glance at the old man. Bobby Jack Wilkes sat stone-faced, blue-lipped, too scared to move or speak. Levi Skoda, although Kiowa couldn't see him, was no doubt in the back of the wagon dreaming morbidly of *La Morte* in the tarot.

Amilia Rathmore reluctantly unlocked Vitto's chains. The fat man hauled himself to his feet, keeping a worried gaze on his father.

"Vitto," Ott Montford snarled, "you're a fool."

Jessie, seeing how the old man was headed, stepped in quickly and grabbed Kiowa's revolver and rifle. Ott lurched forward and slashed the older son across the mouth with the back of his hand. Vitto cowered back against the wagon as the old man hit him again and again across the face.

The old man stood panting, the squirrel rifle under his left arm, rubbing the knuckles of his right hand. Vitto, bowed over, his arms covering his face, still cringed against the wagon. "A fool!" Ott Montford said again. "The good Lord knows I've carried more'n my just load these many years. One son that was fiddle-footed, another one that's just plain lazy and no-account. But worse of all is a fool." He stepped back, diverting some of his anger into other channels. "Wipe your face and stop your blubberin'," he told Vitto. "We got ourselves another fish to fry."

Now, at last, the old man turned his attention to Bobby Jack Wilkes. "This the one?"

Vitto, wiping his bloody mouth on his sleeve, nodded.

The old man glanced at Amilia Rathmore. "Turn him loose."

Jessie shrugged out of his loop of rope; rough hemp, farm rope, nothing that any self-respecting cowhand would have on his saddle. Kiowa, sidling toward the rear of the wagon, heard himself saying, "You're bitin' off more'n you can chew an' swallow, Montford. You can't get away with lynchin' a government prisoner."

Foolishness, nothing but foolishness, every word. They could and would get away with it. Of course, it would come to a bit more than merely hanging a professional assassin. To make the job complete, to get away clean, the Montfords would also have to kill the witnesses—Kiowa, Miss Rathmore, even the crippled hunky in the back of the wagon. An unpleasant necessity, and there wasn't much chance that Ott would baulk at going through with it.

Once again, in the tone of a man who has had his fill of reluctant females, the old man rasped, "I don't aim to say it again, ma'am. Let the prisoner go."

Amilia Rathmore looked to Kiowa, and Kiowa, with a roaring void where his belly ought to be, swallowed and nodded for her to release the assassin.

Bobby Jack began to blubber. "Fod God's sake, you can't let them do this, Jones!"

Jessie laughed. Even Vitto managed a fat-lipped grin. Nothing changed in Ott Montford's face, except that the coals of hate behind his eyes glowed a little brighter. Bobby Jack held his breath, staring wide-eyed at Kiowa, as though expecting a miracle. There was an instant of stark silence disturbed only by Levi Skoda's restless stirring in the wagon.

Miss Rathmore unlocked the prisoner's irons. "Please . . ." she started to beg. Then she looked at the Montford faces, and the concentrated hate seemed to strike her dumb. She turned quickly and closed her eyes as Jessie and Vitto jerked the struggling assassin to his feet.

"Jones, don't let them do it!"

Kiowa hesitated a moment, testing his own temper. Then, as quietly impersonal as a professional hangman, he said, "There's nothin' I can do for you, Wilkes. Your string's played out, face up to it. Take your medicine like a man."

The assassin gasped. The Montfords looked surprised, then grimly amused at the quick turnabout. Amilia Rathmore wheeled and fixed Kiowa with a shocked stare. "How can you say such a thing, when you're bound to protect your prisoner with your life, if need be!"

Kiowa shook his head, unmoved. "He's not my prisoner; I'm just a fellow that happened along at a bad time and offered a hand. And I'm not bound to protect that pretty-faced killer, with my life or anything else." He turned to Ott Montford, shedding his responsibilities with a shrug. "The prisoner's yours, old man, as far as I'm concerned. I don't aim to try to stop you."

Ott Montford's smile was like a freeze cleavage in a block of granite. "Now you're showin' some sense, cowhand. Too bad my own boy don't learn as fast." He gestured to his sons with a grim jerk of his head. "All right, let's don't put it off any longer."

Jessie and Vitto dragged Bobby Jack, hysterical with fear, to a live oak tree at the edge of the brush. They held the prisoner's hands behind his back and recuffed them. Jessie, with a flourish, lobbed the hemp rope over a limb and went to work on the knot.

"Jones, stop them!" the assassin cried. "I'll pay you! I'll make you a rich man! Just don't let them do this!"

Kiowa turned his back on the killer's pleas, and Amilia Rathmore's scorn, and casually built a cigarette. "No, sir," he said to Ott Montford, who was hanging back to keep a watchful eye on the wagon, as well as the hanging. "No, sir, I don't aim to go and get myself killed on *his* account."

"And I thought you had *nerve*!" Amilia Rathmore hissed under her breath. "I thought you were a *man*!"

Ott Montford laughed abruptly with the barking sound of a coyote baying at the moon. Kiowa cringed but kept his face expressionless. "If you don't mind, old man, I'll kind of look the other way. I don't mind tellin' you I ain't got the stomach for lynchin'."

Montford barked again. "All right, cowhand, you don't have to watch if you don't want to." Then, in a raised voice, to his sons: "Get that loop around his neck, Vitto. We won't bother jumpin' him off a horse. Just yank him off the ground and let him kick."

Amilia made a strange keening sound and covered her eyes with her arm. Kiowa moved up to the rear wagon wheel, struck a match on the steel tyre and lit his cigarette. "Let me know when it's over," he told the old man.

"You'll know," Montford said harshly. "You'll know, all right."

Bobby Jack let out a piercing scream as the hemp fell around his neck. Ott Montford, his face a stone mask, turned his attention to the business at hand. "Let's watch him dance!" he shouted. "Pull on that rope, Vitto!"

Kiowa eased to the rear of the wagon. Levi Skoda, as though he had been reading his mind, hauled Amilia Rathmore's ancient Winchester out of a pile of bedding and thrust it into Kiowa's hands.

Bobby Jack screamed again, but the sound was shut off almost immediately. "Stop it!" Kiowa yelled, his voice sounding strange and taut, like the twang of a fiddle string that's about to snap.

Old man Montford turned, his face a mask of rage. Kiowa yelled again. "Drop that rifle, old man. And tell your boys to drop the rope."

For an answer, Ott Montford snarled and swung his long-barrelled rifle on Kiowa. Miss Rathmore's Winchester bellowed and bucked in Kiowa's hands.

It was strange, and frightening, the way the old man seemed to shrink at the instant of death. Suddenly he was no longer the fearsome, hate-filled Ott Montford; he was just a little old man, thin, almost frail, reeling under the impact of the bullet. Then he was down on all fours, bleeding from the mouth and chest, and he looked at Kiowa in a dumb surprise and slowly began to crumble. In a matter of seconds he was dead.

"Let go the rope!" Kiowa yelled at the brothers. It seemed that shouting and yelling was the only way he could speak. "You hear me? Let him down!" He threatened them with the rifle.

Slowly, the stunned brothers eased the dangling Bobby Jack to the ground. The assassin fell to his knees, sputtering, strangling, unable to loosen the knot. Kiowa jogged toward the hanging tree, watchful of the brothers. "Back away! Don't go for your guns!" Again yelling. Forgetting that Vitto was unarmed and Jessie had rested his rifle against the live oak trunk. "Put up your hands!" The stunned men put up their hands, and Kiowa jerked the revolver out of Jessie's waistband. Then, and only then, did he move to Bobby Jack and remove the noose.

"He killed Pa," Vitto said, almost in a whisper. There was awe in the words. He turned to Kiowa, blinking his disbelief. "You killed Pa."

"He didn't leave me any choice." At last he had stopped shouting.

"You didn't have to kill him!" Jessie blurted, his voice cracking. A single tear formed and slipped wetly down the younger brother's face. "Damn you, Jones, you didn't have to go and kill him!"

Suddenly Kiowa Jones was older than his years, tireder than any man had a right to be, and sick in his soul. "I think I had to kill him," he said to himself, silently. "I think I had to, but I'm not sure, and I guess I never will be." Aloud, he said: "Start for the wagon. You too, Wilkes. You've still got a spell to go before you hang."

CHAPTER EIGHT

HATE HAD GONE from them, gushed out of them like life pouring out of an open wound. The Montfords were sick and grieving men with a dead father. Vitto, the fat one, was the picture of dumb shock. Jessie wept openly as they wrapped their pa in a piece of wagon sheeting and rolled him across his saddle. "You'll pay for this, Jones," Jessie said. "You'll pay for this good."

But without the old man they were nothing. They knew it and Kiowa knew it. A war party without a chief. A pit-bull without its fangs. They were nothing. So Kiowa let them go, partly because he knew that he had nothing to fear from them, partly because he felt sorry for them, but mostly because they reminded him of the little old man that he had killed. He wanted them out of his sight.

Bobby Jack was beginning to get it through his mind that he wasn't going to die after all, he wasn't going to hang, at least not yet, and soon he was his old scheming, cocky, deadly self again. "Jones, you're loco, you're crazy, turnin' them Montfords loose like that. They'll come back. You know that, don't you? And you'll pay, all of us will, just like Jessie said."

"Shut up," Kiowa said coldly. He shoved the prisoner to the ground and chained him again to the wagon wheel. "If it wasn't for you, Wilkes, that old man would still be alive. And so would his boy that you killed over in the Panhandle. And I don't feel so good about the whole thing, so if I was you I'd just sit there dumb as a gatepost and not say another word. You hear me?"

Bobby Jack narrowed his eyes but wisely held his tongue. This was not the same free-living, loose-thinking cowhand who, just a short time ago, had blundered into the plague camp on the Washita. Here was a man who had killed, had grown a thick layer of toughness in a short time. Looks could be deceiving. This gangling former grub-line rider, when pushed, could be as dangerous as a wild range cow getting her first sniff of a branding fire. It took an animal-like cunning to know just when to press your luck and when to back away. Bobby Jack Wilkes shrugged and backed away.

Kiowa moved to the back of the wagon and studied the little hunky with mixed emotions. "I can't decide just how to take you, Levi. How'd you know to have that rifle ready just at the right time? You didn't see *that* in your hoodoo cards."

Levi smiled faintly. "I could hear what was happenin', even if I couldn't see. It was no great trick to account for all the guns, except one, the one that belongs to Miss Rathmore, here in the wagon. I figured you'd think of it too."

Kiowa sighed. "The debt's gettin' too heavy on my end, Levi. I owe you more than I can ever pay back. You know that, don't you?"

Levi's smile widened, a gipsy smile, a Skodaschinski smile, a smile that had nothing to do with happiness or pleasure. "Don't worry about it, Jones. There's just one card in the deck for me. You couldn't do anything to change that."

Kiowa walked away from the wagon, into the brush. But that didn't help. Being alone was no good, thinking and stewing and worrying over what had happened, none of it was any good. Ott Montford was still dead—that fact wouldn't change.

After a while Amilia Rathmore came into the brush, worry and concern showing in her face. " Mr. Jones, I'm sorry for the things I said. I'm a silly woman. I hope you can forgive me."

Kiowa turned and looked at her without really seeing her. " I've been thinkin', about that old man. He was haywire, I know that now. Wild as an old brush bull in a loco patch, because of his boy, I guess. But I killed him. I don't know what else I could of done."

She studied his craggy, bearded face.

" Do you believe me, Miss Rathmore?"

" I do, Mr. Jones."

" You think I had a right to kill that old man?"

" It was a necessity, a grim necessity. A problem in human life reduced to simple arithmetic, Mr. Jones. If the Montfords had been allowed to hang Mr. Wilkes, then they would have had to kill us as witnesses to their crime. Four lives against one. It's amazing how much of life can be reduced to simple sums, Mr. Jones."

Kiowa wasn't certain that he understood or was satisfied with her answer, but it was the best he was likely to get. He glanced up at the brilliant sky, seeing for the first time that the day was full light, the prairie so green that it made a man ache just to look at it.

" It's mornin' already. I better go hitch the team."

" Hadn't you better get some rest?"

He rubbed his eyes and the sparkling bristles on his face. " Time for rest later. With a little luck we can make the Choctaw Nation before nightfall."

: : :

They travelled generally east and a little north, following the river that bounded the Chickasaw Nation on the south bank and the Seminole country on the north. Now and then they raised an Indian farm, a slow-moving hack in the distance with a plume of red dust lifting up behind it, occasionally an Indian family walking across the prairie, going Lord knew where.

Toward noon they stopped and boiled coffee and cooked a turkey that Kiowa had shot earlier. It was a foolish thing, risking the chance of exposing their position with useless gunfire, but for the moment Kiowa didn't care.

Nothing came of the turkey hunt except dark, juicy meat on blackjack spits. Old-timers claimed that men who didn't care led charmed lives.

A short while before sundown they glimpsed the Creek Nation over on the north bank, and a few minutes later crossed into the Choctaw Nation on the south side. They circled around the settlement of Leader and pushed on northeast toward the town of South Canadian, one of the several Katy water and fuel stops.

Riding alongside the wagon, Kiowa cast a glance at Bobby Jack. The young assassin, tired of eating dust thrown up by the wagon wheels, had pulled his bandanna up over his nose and mouth. "Jones, I can't sit this saddle much longer without some rest!"

Kiowa, in no mood to listen to Bobby Jack's whining, motioned Amilia Rathmore toward a stand of tall cottonwoods in the distance. "We'll camp there to-night. Maybe to-morrow we can make it on to South Canadian."

Miss Rathmore frowned. "Where?"

"A Katy station to the east of here."

During the day they had pushed into an area of red sandstone hills, which later would flatten out to another strip of prairie that lay at the foot of the Ozark Plateau. Kiowa, a plainsman all his life, had no love for hill country, and with a little luck there would be no need to push into the High Country or, to the south, the Ouachitas.

"What did you say about a Katy station?" Amilia Rathmore asked, after they had cleared a camping space along the river.

"Town by the name of South Canadian, maybe another

day from here," Kiowa told her. "Not much of a place the last time I saw it, but we ought to be able to get word to a government marshal from there." McAlester, a railroad and coal mining town, was closer, but it was too big for Kiowa's liking. Sizable towns only meant more bounty hunters.

Kiowa watered the horses and put them out to graze not far from the wagon. Bobby Jack, a sullen, sweaty, dirty young assassin, was also staked out at his usual spot, the rear wheel of the wagon. Amilia Rathmore, who had been unusually silent as she cooked supper at a smoky pulpwood fire, suddenly asked, "This town of South Canadian, is that where our journey is meant to terminate?"

"End of the line, if that's what you mean. That's where I aim to let go of these prisoners, and not a minute too soon, either."

"But we're almost halfway to Fort Smith. Do you intend to give up that thousand-dollar reward?"

Kiowa shot her a cautious look. "I told that federal deputy, Duncan, that I didn't want that money. And I didn't. And I still don't."

She stabbed slabs of dry-salt with a case knife, turning the meat in the iron skillet. Kiowa noticed spots of colour high on her cheeks and determined little lines at the corners of her mouth. It was surprising, in a way, that he hadn't noticed before, but Amilia Rathmore, all things considered, including the thick-lensed spectacles, wasn't actually a bad-looking woman. Not that this discovery moved Kiowa one way or the other. All women meant to him was rough jokes in a border saloon, some loud laughs and hard whisky, and maybe a little horseplay on the side. That's the way it was when you were a loner riding herd on the other man's stock—the way it had always been, the way he wanted to keep it.

"Give a holler when supper's ready," he said, and walked off to have another look at the horses, which were in tall grass and doing fine without any help from him.

: : : :

Perversely, after almost forty hours of staying awake, Kiowa found that when he closed his eyes that night sleep would not come. Muscles jumped, his mind was restless with fatigue. Swearing hoarsely, he kicked off his bedroll, stamped into his boots and walked off a piece to build a smoke. Bobby Jack Wilkes slept on the ground beside the wagon, as relaxed and guilt-free as a young puma. Levi Skoda snored fitfully on the other side of the wagon, where Kiowa had placed him for the night. Amilia Rathmore, presumably, was sleeping in her accustomed place inside the wagon. But Kiowa Jones, who a few days ago hadn't known the meaning of worry, found his brain crammed with so many frets and frustrations that sleep couldn't find a place to settle down.

"Mr. Jones . . .?"

Her voice startled him. He had been sitting there for several minutes, on a knotty washed-up log, staring into the glistening darkness of the South Canadian River, and she had come up behind him, silent as a possum in a hen-roost. He turned, demanding angrily, "Why ain't you sleepin'?"

"Why aren't you?" she asked, with just a suggestion of frost.

Kiowa shrugged.

"Try not to worry about Mr. Montford. It wasn't your fault."

"Who said I was worryin'?" he almost snarled. "And who said I thought it was my fault?"

Amilia Rathmore blinked nearsightedly. "I'm sorry . . . I thought . . ." She let the words trail off. Kiowa stared at her. He had never seen a woman in such a getup. She looked surprisingly small, and different, almost like a schoolgirl instead of a teacher, bundled from chin to the ground in some sort of pale, bulky wrap-around, a ridiculous nightcap almost falling off the back of her head. She wasn't wearing her spectacles—maybe that was what made the difference.

She looked slightly angry but not particularly self-conscious or embarrassed at appearing before a relative stranger in her nightdress—if that's what it was. "I don't mean to be a nuisance, Mr. Jones, but there's something I feel needs discussing."

"What?" Kiowa demanded bluntly.

"Well . . ." She made a meaningless gesture with one hand. For the first time since Kiowa had known her she was at a loss for words. She cleared her throat and started again. "Well, for one thing there's the matter of the reward. That thousand dollars is rightfully yours, and you will have earned it, if you succeed in handing Mr. Wilkes over to the authorities at Fort Smith. It would be folly not to accept it."

Kiowa squinted, downing an impulse to growl. "Folly," he said dryly. "Well, you may be right at that. I ain't above makin' a mistake now and again. But I already made up my mind about that money: I don't want it, I ain't goin' to take it, and I sure don't aim to haze these prisoners all the way to Arkansas."

An icy silence built up between them. "Mr. Jones," she said at last, "do you have any idea . . . any idea at all, what you could do with a thousand dollars?"

"Sure." Kiowa grinned wolfishly. "I could drink all the whisky I could hold, make some monte or faro dealer happy, and maybe outfit some saloon girl with flounces and ostrich feathers, and two days later I'd have nothin' but empty pockets and the world's champion headache. That's just what would happen—I can see it as clear as the hunky can see his own hangin' in that hoodoo deck of his, and I don't figure it's somethin' to risk gettin' killed for."

He got up from the log and added, in a tone meant to end the discussion, "So now you know why the idea of a thousand dollars don't work me up the way it might with some other gent." He touched his tattered hatbrim with cool cow-country politeness. "Good night, Miss Rathmore."

She stood there for several seconds, a pale, squinting statue, then suddenly she wheeled and almost ran back to the wagon. Kiowa heaved a bone-aching sigh. He built another smoke, but it was hot and tasteless and he stamped it out on the ground. Women! He returned to his roll and sometime in the early morning, as the dew began to settle, fell into a fitful sleep.

: :   : :

The next day they rattled north-eastward, skirting an Indian village on the Choctaw side of the river, a place called Shawnee Town. Soon they were in the Prairie Plains country, the last strip of easy travelling between the Wichitas and the Ozark Plateau.

Kiowa, riding alongside the wagon, called up to Amilia Rathmore. "Sometime to-morrow we ought to raise South Canadian. Not much of a haul on to Tahlequah. Thought I might ride on a piece in that direction, after I get the prisoners off my hands . . . if you don't mind some company."

She stared down at him through her thick lenses. "You're still bound to throw away that reward money, aren't you?"

Kiowa shrugged self-consciously. "About last night, I guess I spoke a little out of turn. I apologize for that. But you're right about the money; it just ain't that important to me."

Her gaze narrowed. Suddenly she faced straight ahead and cracked the lines over the team. The rest of the day passed in a kind of steely silence that caused Kiowa to twist uncomfortably in the saddle every time he chanced to look in her direction. That's what you got when you tried to talk sense to women. Looks that would freeze the horns off a Dakota steer.

But at least there was no further trouble from the Montfords, and no sign of more bounty hunters dogging their trail. They made camp that night beside a prairie stream, in a pleasant grove of willows and persimmon and jack oak, and it looked like clear sailing ahead. Another day would see them in South Canadian. End of the line. And Kiowa had a last look at the horses, then saw that the prisoners were bedded down and secure for the night. "Looks like we gave the scalp hunters the slip," he offered, picking his teeth with a whittled stick as Amilia Rathmore cleaned the dishes and cooking pots.

She shot him a chilly glance that Kiowa preferred to ignore. "I been thinkin'. There ain't no need of takin' that team and wagon clear to Tahlequah. You can sell the rig in South Canadian, catch the Katy up to Muskogee, then coach it on to Tahlequah. A lot faster and a sight smoother than goin' all the way by wagon."

"You've been thinking," she said bitingly. "Did you think how I was to transport my household goods and school supplies without a wagon?"

Kiowa blinked, scratched his whiskered face, guessing maybe he'd take a few whacks with a razor when they got to South Canadian, if he got around to it. "Well, the Katy runs freight cars. And there's bull and mule trains workin' between Muskogee and Tahlequah . . ."

Amilia Rathmore made an impatient sound as she put away her dishes. "Women don't get rich teaching school, Mr. Jones," she said sarcastically. "Do you have any idea what it would cost to ship my belongings by train and wagon freighters?"

Kiowa hadn't carried the thought quite that far. Anyhow, he hadn't meant anything in particular. Just trying to keep things friendly until the trip was over. But if she was so dead set against it. . . . Kiowa heaved himself to his feet and with a stiff nod started toward his roll.

"Mr. Jones . . ."

He hesitated, looked back, and she said, "I didn't mean to snap at you. I'm sorry."

Kiowa grinned. "Sure. This thing's startin' to rub our fur the wrong way, I guess. But it won't be for much longer."

"I suppose not. . . ." She hesitated, struggling with her feminine pride. At last she said, "The coffee's still hot, Mr. Jones . . ."

The tension eased. Kiowa hunkered by the fire, blowing on his coffee, watching her with a kind of dim curiosity. For a while he listened to the breeze in the lacy willows, watched the swooping bull bats overhead, their white-striped wings catching the last light of dusk. He thought of all the times he'd lain out in the open this way, living with the wild things, thinking about that *someday* of the future when he'd do his sleeping in a house, his own house, with his own roof over his head. It was a thought that plagued all cowhands at one time or another, and usually that's all it ever came to—a thought, a wish.

Amilia Rathmore was saying quietly, almost to herself, " I think I can understand the attraction of a nomadic life, Mr. Jones. If I were a man, perhaps I would choose such a life for myself." She smiled faintly. " Perhaps that is the reason I've tried so hard to find fault with it, because it's something I can't have."

Kiowa showed signs of surprise. " It's the first time I ever heard a woman own up to it. I mean, most women, if it's somethin' they can't have, they usually want to tramp on it."

Amilia Rathmore's eyes widened behind her spectacles. Kiowa didn't notice. He was too busy being cocksure of himself to notice much of anything, even the snap of a dry willow twig from somewhere downstream.

For several minutes the two of them sat beside the fire, Miss Rathmore on a sack of shelled corn, Kiowa hunkering Southwest-fashion on his heels. At last Miss Rathmore asked, with a touch of nervousness, " I'm curious, Mr. Jones. I understand how the wanderer's life might be desirable for a young man, or "—pointedly—" or even a man your own age. But I can't help wondering. What does a man do when he is too old to play the vagabond, when sleeping in the open makes his bones ache, when he can no longer sit a saddle or do hard labour for stretches of eighteen to twenty hours? How does a man, a man like yourself, Mr. Jones, prepare himself for the future?" This last so condescending and slathered with sweetness that even a man of Kiowa's blunt nature was capable of understanding it.

He felt himself flushing, partly because it was none of her business, partly because he didn't like being hazed by a woman . . . but mostly his discomfiture came from the knowledge that he could offer no answers to her impertinent questions. No reasonable answers. And he couldn't bring himself to admit that he had sometimes asked the same questions of himself.

He resorted to the only defence a man could use, when he had no defence. He attacked.

" Well, now," he said, borrowing some of her own syrupy sweetness, " a man takes his future as it comes, that's the way

I see it. And he watches out that some female don't get her loop around his neck and drags him over to a brandin' fire. There's females like that, I hear."

She smiled and nodded. Kiowa grinned pleasantly. And anger danced between them like fox fire in a thunderstorm.

A heavy, flat-heeled boot tramped an acorn a scant fifty yards from the campfire. This time Kiowa heard it. Suddenly there was a loud hammering in his chest. His scalp prickled. What if it was Vitto and Jessie Montford returning to settle for their pa's killing? What if it was another money killer intent on Bobby Jack's double bounty? A dozen possibilities flashed through Kiowa's mind, all of them bad.

Instinct set Kiowa in action, jerked him from his hunkering position and threw him recklessly at the startled Amilia Rathmore. They crashed to the ground, Miss Rathmore gasping, the breath driven from her lungs. Kiowa grabbed her arm and dragged her unchivalrously into the shadow of the wagon. At the same time he had managed to claw his revolver from his waistband and point it in the general direction of the sound.

"Come in with your hands up, mister! I mean business!"

Amilia Rathmore twisted out of his grasp and stared at him as if he had gone mad.

"Easy on that trigger, friend," a voice called from the darkness. "It's just me, old Rupe Dobie."

A look of grudging respect showed in Miss Rathmore's glance at Kiowa. "Who is he? Do you know him?"

"Never heard of him," Kiowa grunted. Then, in a raised voice, "Come on in, mister, where we can get a look at you."

With a measured, procession-like stride, the man stepped out of the night into the circle of firelight. He carried his hat in his hand and his bald head shone like polished bone. His eyes were lost in deep sockets beneath bushy brows, his nose was thin and hooked like an eagle's beak, his mouth was loose and moist and red—or maybe that was a trick of the firelight.

"I seen your fire, friend, and smelled your coffee, and I says to myself, 'Now these good folks wouldn't begrudge old Rupe Dobie . . .'"

"What's your business?" Kiowa demanded.

"Business? Well, now . . ." He rubbed his jutting chin and seemed vaguely amused. "You never heard my name? Rupe Dobie?"

"No." But that wasn't quite the truth. In the back of Kiowa's mind the name struck an uneasy note. "I ask you again, mister. What's your business?"

"Well . . ." the man sighed, "if you just got to know . . ." He stepped in closer, glimpsed the sullen Bobby Jack Wilkes chained to the wagon wheel, and left his sentence hanging. His mouth moved loosely in what might have been a grin, speckled teeth flashing in the firelight. "I've seen that face before, young man. Could it have been on a 'wanted poster' maybe? The kind they circulate around the government courts?"

Kiowa tensed. "Don't get any fancy notions, mister. It's been hard luck and a fast funeral so far, for them that's come after the Wilkes bounty, and there's no reason to think you'd come off any better."

Rupe Dobie made a hollow sound of disbelief. "That young lad's the famous Bobby Jack Wilkes? It ain't possible!"

Kiowa scowled. If Rupe wasn't a bounty hunter, what was he? He was no Indian. He didn't look like the common run of saddle bum, and he wasn't dressed fancy enough for a peddler. He seemed to be unarmed and afoot—a dangerous combination in this country.

"It just ain't possible!" he said again, under his breath. Bobby Jack squirmed uneasily under Dobie's dark gaze.

"Get him away from here, Jones. I ain't no baboon in a circus cage."

Rupe Dobie laughed softly. "Yes, sir, it's young Wilkes, all right. I should of knowed right off." He glanced at Kiowa.

"It's providential, Marshal! That's what it is, providential!"

All through the aimless exchange the name of Dobie had been rattling in Kiowa's mind, like a roulette ball looking for the right slot to fall into. Suddenly it dropped. The name clicked.

Amilia Rathmore, seeing the expression on Kiowa's face, became alarmed.

"Mr. Jones, what is it?"

Kiowa put away his revolver, sighing. "I just pegged our visitor. Rupe Dobie. I've heard the name often enough; but I guess I never expected to meet him face to face. You've heard about old Izaac Parker, over at Fort Smith, haven't you?"

She nodded uncertainly. "The Hanging Judge, as they call him?"

"He's the one. Well . . ." Kiowa sounded as though the word hurt. "The gent standin' there in front of us, Rupe Dobie, he's old Parker's chief executioner, the hangman that invented the Fort Smith hanging machine that can string up a dozen men at one whack."

Miss Rathmore's face became curiously stiff. "Why has he come here? What does he want?"

"Lord knows," Kiowa groaned under his breath.

Dobie, smiling his lax smile, only half listened to the taut exchange between Kiowa and Amilia Rathmore. He studied Bobby Jack with the rapt gaze of a gem thief inspecting the crown jewels. The assassin gaped, suspended for the moment in that lonesome place between panic and rage.

"Young man," Dobie asked with chill formality, "would you please draw back your shoulders, lift your chin just a little . . .?"

"Jones, I ain't goin' to stand for this! Get this buzzard away from me!"

Kiowa got to his feet. His words, aimed at the hangman, were almost as angry as the assassin's. "I want some straight talk, Dobie. What're you doin' here? How'd you know where to find us?"

"Friend," the hangman droned in a voice that seemed to come from the bottom of a stone cistern, "I didn't know anything about you. Like I said, it's providential. My mule pulled up lame, maybe a mile south of here, and I saw your campfire. There ain't anything to fret about, Marshal. We're on the same side of the law, ain't we?"

With forced patience, Kiowa explained once more that he was no marshal, that he was merely a cowhand who had fallen into a job that he didn't like and didn't want and intended to rid himself of as soon as possible. "Which," he added, "will be to-morrow, the way I figure it, when we get to South Canadian and somebody sends for a real marshal."

Rupe Dobie wagged his head, looking as if he might be in pain. "Friend, that valuable prisoner of yours wouldn't last no time at all in South Canadian, nor any other settlement along the railroad. Every white man in the Territory, and maybe some of the Indians, is lookin' to land hisself that double bounty by takin' Wilkes out of the law's hands. My advice to you is head straight for Fort Smith, and don't stop at any settlement between here and the Arkansas line."

Suddenly Kiowa Jones felt years older than he had a few minutes before.

"Speakin' of Fort Smith," the hangman said offhandedly, "I'll just travel along that way with you, if you don't mind."

CHAPTER NINE

It was a bad night all around. Kiowa loaned Dobie the spare saddle horse, the grey gelding, to ride back and pick up his plunder. While the hangman was gone the wind began to rise. A heavy cloud bank rolled in from the west and smothered the moon. The prairie lay in darkness and the soggy air was shot with electric stillness. "I can see right now," Kiowa muttered, "the stretch between here and day-break ain't goin' to be no bed of roses."

For one thing, Amilia Rathmore decided to work herself up to a worrying frame of mind. "Mr. Jones. I don't like that man, Mr. Dobie. I don't trust him. Are you sure it's wise to take him into camp and allow him to associate with the prisoners?"

"I ain't sure of anything," Kiowa said between his teeth. "But Rupe Dobie's a legal officer of a United States court, and I don't guess it would be smart to get his back up any more'n we can help."

Miss Rathmore blinked rapidly and turned her face from the firelight.

Bobby Jack Wilkes began to yell. "Jones, I ain't goin' to stand for it, I tell you! I ain't goin' to be cooped up with no buzzard of a hangman. You hear me?"

Kiowa wheeled and glared at the prisoner. "You just keep your mouth shut," he snarled.

In the back of the wagon Levi Skoda groaned and called, "Jones, I'm parched. I want some water."

Kiowa hauled down the wagon canteen. It was empty. In a burst of temper, he kicked the wagon wheel and swore.

"Mr. Jones!" Amilia Rathmore said in a pained tone.

Kiowa thrust the canteen into her hands. "Get some water from the creek," he commanded. She stared wide-eyed for an instant, then wheeled and scurried away in the direction of the stream. Off to the west lightning began to stab through the rolling thunderheads. The spring storm charged the atmosphere with electricity; it made the skin itch, the palms sweat, it rubbed tempers to a jagged edge.

Skoda, who never complained, was complaining for the second time in as many minutes. "Jones, can't I even get a drink of water? Don't I get any consideration at all? It ain't like I never done *you* any favours."

Kiowa stuck his head in the back of the wagon and snapped, "Shut up, Skoda. I'm sick of listenin' to your whinin'!"

He knew that he was not being reasonable, that the tensions were largely the results of the stifling atmosphere that raced ahead of the night storm. The first clap of thunder rumbled over the prairie like some giant runaway bull train.

"Jones!" Bobby Jack howled. "Unlock these chains! Let me loose from here!"

"One more word out of you," Kiowa said with a softness that fooled no one, "and a rainstorm will be the least of your worries."

The first heavy raindrop struck Kiowa between the shoulders. He scrambled up to the wagon box and began pulling the sheet over the front bows. He slipped, skinning his knuckles on the break lever, but managed to close the sheet. The leading edge of the storm swept toward them. Raindrops fell singly, thudding against the taut canvas. Kiowa found a lantern, lit it and swung it from one of the middle bows. Then, on a sudden inspiration, he began searching the front end of the wagon.

Miss Rathmore raised the sheet, handing the filled canteen up to Kiowa, just as the raindrops stopped falling singly and began coming down in heavy clusters. Kiowa took the canteen with one hand. With the other hand he tilted Amilia Rathmore's jug of fiery whisky and swigged from the neck.

"Mr. Jones!"

Kiowa grinned, wiping his mouth on his sleeve. "Guess I never did learn how to resist temptation. Anyhow we can rest a little easier, now that the storm's broke. Let me give you a hand."

Haughtily, she declined the offer and climbed into the wagon box by herself.

Bobby Jack yelped, "Goddammit, Jones, I'll drown out here!"

Wearily, Kiowa slid the whisky jug under the wagon seat and climbed down to the ground. Lightning split the boiling cloud cover, and a moment later thunder clapped overhead like a brass Napoleon. Rupe Dobie, bouncing with scarecrow gracelessness, broke out of the brush astride the grey gelding. As Kiowa unlocked Bobby Jack's irons, the hangman peeled the rig from the grey's back and flung it under the wagon, then he tied the animal on the lee of the wagon and climbed in the back end with Levi Skoda.

"Get in," Kiowa ordered, indicating the back of the wagon with a jab of his chin.

The assassin shrunk back. "Not me! I ain't settin' jowl by jowl with no hangman!"

Already soaked to the skin, his patience exhausted, Kiowa grabbed the killer's arm and started to lock him back to the wheel. Bobby Jack had a fast second thought and relented.

He climbed in and Kiowa wrapped his chains around one of the sturdy oak bows and locked them. The wind was howling, the rain slashing like knives as Kiowa closed the puckered opening in the back of the wagon and climbed over the hill of household goods to sit up front with Amilia Rathmore.

When the wind seized the wagon and rocked it dangerously, Miss Rathmore showed that she could be frightened like any other woman. She grasped Kiowa's arm and held it tightly. Rupe Dobie, crouching atop a dismantled kitchen stove, grinned loosely at Kiowa.

"How about it, friend—you think this storm'll last long?"

"Long enough," Kiowa muttered, "to drive our horses clear to the Brazos, if they pull their stake pins."

The hangman sighed unworriedly and lay back on his elbow. Bobby Jack shrunk back against the wagon box, getting as far from Dobie as possible, eyeing the hangman glassily. From time to time Dobie would cast a thoughtful, half-amused glance in the assassin's direction, and Bobby Jack would turn white and freeze.

"May I ask, young man," Dobie asked with dry politeness, "how old you are?"

Bobby Jack gazed dumbly at the hangman's eyes. Dobie wiped his loose lips with the back of his hand. "It don't really matter." He shrugged. "Of course, for a perfect job, a man can't be too careful. Every detail must be considered. But there's time enough for that . . . later."

The young assassin looked sick, but he was caught in the hangman's spell. "Let's see," Rupe Dobie murmured placidly, as though to himself. "Let's have a look at you, Mr. Wilkes." He sized up Bobby Jack with a practised eye. "Age twenty, maybe twenty-one or two. Weight, eleven stone, give or take a couple of pounds." He assumed the mildly superior air of an educator. "That comes to a hundred and fifty pounds or thereabouts, the way we reckon weight in this country. I favour the British system myself—Britishers've been at hangin' longer'n man can tell, so they say. Got it down to a gnat's whisker, artistic-like." His bald head waggled in admiration. "Say what you like about Britishers as folks, but as hangmen there ain't no better."

Miss Rathmore's hand tightened on Kiowa's arm. He turned, looking at Dobie, and said coldly, "Don't you get enough of that at Fort Smith?"

The hangman shrugged. "Hangin's like any other business, friend. You get out of it what you put in it, like they say. I try to do a good job. There ain't nothin' wrong with that, is there?"

"I can't say, and I'd rather not hear any more about it."

Rupe Dobie sighed with an injured air and spread his hands in a gesture of surrender. For a few minutes the crowded wagon occupants listened to the howling wind and the rain drumming against the tightly drawn canvas. The lantern glowed rosily against the underside of the tarp.

Prairie storms didn't last long, as a rule, but while they did last they could do the damage of a full stampede. Kiowa, with one ear tuned to every shift and gust of the wind, was earnestly hoping that their horses would stay satisfied in the protected draw where he had staked them. Amilia Rathmore huddled on the wagon seat, clutching at Kiowa's arm, finding something there that was stronger than the feminine security that she had built for herself with so much care over the years. Levi Skoda, his face flushed with fever, lay back and closed his eyes and thought of that day, not far away, when the long sleep would take him, and the ghost of Amabel would not pursue him. As for Bobby Jack Wilkes—all of his senses were drawn to the hangman. No matter how he tried, he could not turn his frightened eyes away.

Then Rupe Dobie said in a conversational tone, as though his grim monologue had never been interrupted, "Yes, sir, friend, the Britishers they got it worked out to a *T*. Take our young friend here, Mr. Wilkes. A London hangman would have him pegged in a wink. Weight eleven stone, five. Height five-nine. No unusual muscular development of the neck or shoulder. A good, angular jaw to set the brass eye against, layin' the knot alongside the left ear. No problems at all. A hangman couldn't ask for no better client, like they say, than Mr. Wilkes." He did a bit of rapid calculation in his head. "Nine feet, three inches!" he announced proudly. "That's what the drop will be for Mr. Wilkes."

Rupe Dobie smiled pleasantly at the hostile faces. "That's the Britishers for you, right down to a gnat's whisker. What they've done," he explained comfortably, "is work out a table of drops that never misses—well, *almost* never. They take a man weighin' eighteen stone, and they know that such a man, with normal neck and muscular development—know it from a hundred years of study and experimentin'—they know he'll want a drop of just eight feet. On the dot. So usin' that as a basis, you might say, they worked it out that for every half-stone lighter weight, it takes a two-inch longer drop. It does the job every time. Almost." He snapped his fingers to indicate a neat, workmanlike break of a spinal column.

Suddenly Bobby Jack began to scream. "I'll kill him! I'll kill him!" He lunged to his knees, pulling savagely at the chains.

Kiowa yelled, "Sit down, Wilkes, and shut up!"

The assassin didn't hear, or at any rate did not heed. He continued to scream threats at the hangman while fighting the chains. Grimly, Kiowa started back over the hills of Miss Rathmore's household goods. As he grabbed for the violent young assassin, a rush of wind roared down through the natural funnel of the creek bottom. The wagon felt strangely light, lifting crazily on the left side. The canvas sheet rippled, then cracked with the sound of a rifle shot as one of the oaken bows was ripped from its iron bracket. Amilia Rathmore screamed. With dreamlike slowness, the wind nudged the wagon over on its side, dumping passengers and goods into the rain and mud.

Kiowa landed on his back, watched the wagon and most of its contents come down on top of him. He scrambled out of the way of the wagon, but a stove lid from Miss Rathmore's wood burner struck him behind the left ear and sent him sprawling. Over the sound of the wind he remembered hearing Amilia Rathmore calling, "Mr. Jones!" Then a darkness blacker than the storm closed in on him.

The next thing he remembered was the taste of mud in his mouth, and rain pelting his face, and Miss Rathmore bending anxiously over him. "Mr. Jones, are you all right?"

He spat mud, cursing under his breath. "How long've I been out?"

"Just a minute." She had lost her spectacles but had somehow grabbed the lantern and kept it from going out. Rain plastered her hair to her head like a skullcap and ran down her face like a solid stream of tears. For one groggy moment Kiowa thought they *were* tears. He pulled himself out of the mud, to his knees. Pain pierced his skull with the sharpness of a hatpin.

"What about the prisoners?" he asked. "They all right?"

She shook her head dumbly. "I . . . don't know. I think so."

"You *think* so!" He lurched to his feet and began ripping away the shredded remains of the wagon sheet. Levi Skoda lay under the wagon box, cushioned on a mound of bedding. Kiowa lifted one corner of the wagon and pulled him out. "You all right, Levi?"

The little hunky nodded, gritting his teeth. The splints on his leg had been pulled out of place, and maybe the leg had been rebroken, for all Kiowa knew. "I'll fix that for you, Levi. In just a minute."

The wind was letting up. The storm was over, but the rain was just beginning. Kiowa blundered through the wreckage by the light of Amilia Rathmore's lantern. Rupe Dobie came limping toward them from the other side of the wagon. He had been thrown clear and was unhurt except for a twisted knee.

"Friend," the hangman announced blithely, leaning on Kiowa's shoulder, "I'm afraid I've got some bad news for you."

"Save it!" Kiowa panted. "Have you seen anything of Wilkes?"

Dobie smiled wetly in the lantern light. "That's what I was goin' to tell you. He's gone. The bow bracket pulled out when the wagon went over, and our Mr. Wilkes got away clean as a whistle."

CHAPTER TEN

KIOWA'S FIRST SENSATION was one of relief. He was glad that Wilkes had got away. Glad he was gone. Glad the storm had come along and solved the problem of what to do with the young killer. No one could blame him for the storm. No one could say that Kiowa Jones hadn't done the right thing and taken more than his rightful share of the responsibility, herding two dangerous prisoners clear from the Washita. But just the same he was glad it was over. Glad that Wilkes was out there somewhere, Lord knew where, in the rain and darkness where it was impossible to track him.

Amilia Rathmore was tugging at his sleeve. " Mr. Jones, what are we going to do?"

He wished folks would stop asking him what to do. He didn't mean to do anything. Except look for a place to get out of the rain and enjoy his new-found freedom from responsibility. " Dobie, give me a hand. Let's see if we can get this wagon back on its wheels."

" Whatever you say, friend. But don't you think you ought to do somethin' about that valuable prisoner of yours?"

" He ain't my prisoner," Kiowa growled. " He's out there somewhere." He waved at the black, wet night. " Runnin' like a buck deer, more'n likely, but who knows in which direction . . .?"

Running. Now it occurred to Kiowa that he had forgotten to replace the assassin's leg irons when he had transferred Wilkes to the wagon. His hands would be cuffed, but that wouldn't mean much to an expert killer and law-dodger like Bobby Jack Wilkes.

" Maybe he ain't runnin' at all," the hangman suggested.

Kiowa scowled.

The three of them huddled around the flickering lantern, more for warmth than for the light, with icy rain flowing down their faces, plastering their muddy clothing to their bodies.

"Reckon I forgot to mention it," Rupe Dobie said conversationally, "but before Wilkes lit out for the brush, he grabbed your rifle. For all we know, he's out there somewhere right now, aimin 'to kill the bunch of us."

Kiowa grabbed the lantern from Amilia Rathmore's hand and placed it well away from the upturned wagon. If Wilkes *was* out there, there wasn't much sense giving him such a good target to shoot at.

When Kiowa returned to the others he looked at Dobie and said in a voice that was colder than the rain, "So you forgot to mention it, did you? Well, you forgot somethin' else. You forgot to tie fast when you left the gelding beside the wagon. The grey's gone."

The hangman nodded but showed no sign of being very disturbed. "That's too bad."

Too bad! "Grab hold of the wagon!" Kiowa growled.

For the next several minutes he worked off some of his anger, struggling in the slippery mud, trying to get the running gears on the ground again. Miss Rathmore, when Kiowa's back was turned, moved the lantern over to Levi Skoda and began replacing the hunky's splints.

At last Kiowa and Dobie wrestled the wagon right side up. They salvaged two bows that hadn't been splintered, jammed them into the brackets and tried to put up some kind of shelter with the shredded wagon sheet. It wasn't much good. The wagon box was full of mud, the sheet was a wreck, but they managed to work out some protection from the wind and driving rain. When the job was finished, Kiowa, in an instinctive action of survival, reached under the wagon seat for the whisky jug.

His fingers touched the sharp edges of the broken vessel. Kiowa groaned. He couldn't have been more shaken if it had been his own blood that had spilled.

It was at that moment, mingled with the sound of driving rain, that he heard the faint, almost inaudible rattle of chains. Coming suddenly erect, Kiowa grabbed for his waistband, but the revolver wasn't there. It had gone into the mud with everything else, lost, maybe, for ever. He threw back the canvas that he and Dobie had been working on, and the first thing he saw was Amilia Rathmore, sharply etched in the diffused light of the spitting lantern, carefully binding Levi Skoda's injured leg.

"Get away from that light!" Kiowa bellowed at the top of his voice, and vaulted down from the wagon. Miss Rathmore looked up, startled. Then Bobby Jack Wilkes stepped into the outer edge of the circle of light, holding Kiowa's rifle awkwardly, but not too awkwardly, with the muzzle pointed directly at Amilia Rathmore.

Rupe Dobie put his head above the top of the wagon box and froze. Kiowa started angrily forward, but after a few impulsive steps came to a rigid standstill.

"Stand steady, cowboy," the assassin snarled, hunching against the biting rain. He stopped when the Winchester's muzzle was no more than a foot from Amilia Rathmore's head. He glanced toward the wagon, at the hangman, and grinned with all of his old savagery. "Come on down, Dobie. Me and you've got a little business together, soon's I get loose from these chains."

Now Kiowa was beginning to understand, and he didn't like it. Wilkes, after a few minutes of blind running, must have realized he didn't have much chance of escape, over the long haul, unless he got free of the chains and handcuffs. So he had returned, knowing just how to manage it—or thinking that he did.

He waited until Rupe Dobie scrambled nervously down from the wagon, then he turned to Kiowa, but kept the rifle aimed at Amilia Rathmore's head. "You know what I want, cowboy. The key to these irons. Throw it over here, nice and easy, right at my feet, and maybe I can be talked out of pullin' this trigger."

Kiowa swallowed, hard, his mouth as dry as winter sage. "Look here," he started indignantly, but saw immediately that the assassin was in no mood to exchange threats. Those wolfish eyes narrowed ever so slightly, and he grasped the rifle just a little tighter.

" It's up to you, Jones. You want Miss Rathmore dead or alive?"

Kiowa licked his lips. It was strange that he could be so hot and dry on the inside when, on the outside, he was so cold and wet. He glanced at Miss Rathmore, but she quickly turned her head, hiding the panic in her eyes. There was nothing to do but give the killer the key. Slowly, Kiowa began reaching for his shirt pocket.

" All right, Wilkes. Any way you want it, but point that rifle somewhere else."

Bobby Jack flashed his wide, mirthless grin. " After I get shed of these chains, cowboy. Now the key . . ."

Kiowa touched his pocket—and an icy finger raked up his back. The key wasn't there. It must have fallen out when the wagon went over. Now it was lost, buried in the slime and mud, like the pistol and everything else. He took a long, deep breath while the assassin's patience neared the jump-off point.

" I told you, Jones!"

Kiowa heard himself saying, " The key's gone. I must of lost it. When the wagon went over." The voice sounded queer and thin, not like his voice at all.

Bobby Jack stared, and then in his own quiet, deadly way, went wild. ". . . All right," he said, so softly that Kiowa could hardly hear him over the sound of the rain. " All right, Jones. If this is the way you want it."

Kiowa could see—or thought he could see—the assassin's trigger finger start its squeeze. " Hold it, Wilkes!" Kiowa fumbled with his pocket, his mind racing in panic, his common sense telling him to cut and run, because it was the only chance he had of seeing his way out of this fix alive. And it wasn't much of a chance at that. Instead, he heard himself saying, " Here's the key!"

He started forward, holding out the hand that was supposed to be holding the key.

" That's close enough!" Bobby Jack snapped. " Throw the key. I'll pick it up all right."

Kiowa pretended not to hear. An unbelievable pretension

—but it was an unbelievable situation. The assassin would never believe that the key was lost, not in a thousand years. Unless his attention was diverted, he would kill Amilia Rathmore as unfeelingly as a steer would tail-whip a heel fly—and probably he would do it anyhow, no matter what anyone did. Kiowa kept coming, figuring there wasn't much to lose for any of them.

"I ain't tellin' you again, Jones. Stop right where you are!"

"Here's your key. You don't want to lose it in the mud, do you?"

Bobby Jack swore under his breath and instinctively turned the rifle from the still target of Amilia Rathmore to Kiowa Jones who was bearing down on him from the other direction. Maybe the action was senseless, but Kiowa learned one thing from it. When Bobby Jack Wilkes issued a warning, he meant what he said. Without giving the matter another thought, the assassin levelled the rifle at Kiowa's chest and pulled the trigger.

The snap sounded as loud as a thunderclap. But it was still a snap. A misfire. Possibly because mud had worked its way into the weapon's action, or maybe the ammunition had gone bad. It could have been any one of a hundred reasons, for a rifle that had been so long mistreated.

Bobby Jack looked startled, unbelieving, when no explosion answered the trigger squeeze. He understood guns and pampered them the way another man might pamper a beautiful woman. A thing like killing, the blotting out of a human life, Bobby Jack understood and accepted without question, but the abuse of a precision instrument of death was beyond his comprehension. It took some time for the truth to sink in, and when it did he snarled his rage and quickly levered another round into the chamber.

Kiowa had already lunged for the killer's legs, attempting to dive under the Winchester's muzzle. This time there was no misfire. Kiowa felt the prick, a bee sting, a little tug at his neck, about two inches below his left ear. He scarcely felt it as he sloughed into the mud and knocked the assassin sprawling.

The rifle flew out of Bobby Jack's hands. Handcuffed as he was, the assassin was unable to keep his balance, and crashed awkwardly into the ooze. In a cold, uncharacteristic fury, Kiowa was on top of the prisoner, grabbed the front of Bobby Jack's mud-smeared shirt and drew back his fist. Something in the back of Kiowa's mind spoke softly—too softly, perhaps: *You can't hit him. He's your prisoner. He's chained and helpless, he's not free to fight back.*

Kiowa hit him anyway, full in the face, calling on all the strength that was in him. The numbing shock in his fist felt good. Nothing had ever felt better.

Then the bee sting in his neck was no longer a mere sting. It felt like a pitch pine splinter driven beneath the skin, Comanche-fashion, and set afire.

He started falling face down in the mud and caught himself on his hands. For a moment he rocked on all fours, like some maddened old range bull getting his first blood-boiling sniff of the slaughter pens. Then, very slowly, his arms and legs gave way and down he went.

"Mr. Jones!"

Amilia Rathmore stood for a moment, frozen, as the blood of Kiowa Jones mingled with the blood-red mud of the Choctaw plains. With considerable effort, she took herself in hand and called, "Mr. Dobie, help me get Mr. Jones under the shelter." When the hangman didn't appear at once, she wheeled toward the wagon. "Mr. Dobie!"

Something in her voice caused Rupe Dobie to leave the relative comfort of the makeshift shelter and brave the slashing rain. The hangman was not an emotional man, but he understood that he would be a dead man at this moment if Jones hadn't done what he had done. There were few things in this life that a condemned man would enjoy as much as killing a hangman—and no one knew that as well as Dobie. He had nothing to fear at the moment, but it had been a near thing. And it had shaken him.

"Mr. Dobie!"

"Right here, Miss Rathmore."

Miss Rathmore was on her knees trying to get a makeshift bandage on the wound. There seemed to be a great deal of blood. Rupe Dobie didn't like to admit it, but he had never had much stomach for blood. Maybe that was why he was such an expert, and careful, hangman.

Between the two of them they wrestled Kiowa into the back of the wagon and dragged him beneath the tattered canvas. "What about Wilkes?" Dobie asked nervously.

"I don't think Mr. Wilkes will be a problem for several minutes yet. Please turn your head, Mr. Dobie."

The hangman blinked, then understood and turned his head while Amilia Rathmore ripped off a length of petticoat. The bullet had missed the big neck artery, but the rush of blood was still alarming. Dobie, strangely pale around the mouth, watched as Miss Rathmore fashioned a compress of white petticoat material and put it to the wound.

"You think he'll live?" the hangman asked worriedly.

"We'll hope so," Amilia Rathmore said in a strange harsh voice. "We'll do all we can. And then we'll pray."

"Maybe I better look after the prisoners," the hangman muttered, crawfishing out of the wagon.

The thing about being a hangman was that death was always for the other fellow. But during these past few minutes death had brushed shoulders with the hangman himself. It was a new experience for Rupe Dobie, and he didn't like it. He didn't like it at all.

CHAPTER ELEVEN

MORNING CAME ON, still and cold and wet as only a prairie morning can be after a heavy storm. At first light Levi Skoda cleared a place beneath the tarp and began laying out the tarot. Rupe Dobie, who had been struggling with wet matches and wetter wood, finally got a fire started with the help of coal oil from Miss Rathmore's lantern. The wagon was a mess, but it did not seem to be seriously damaged except for the canvas. The contents of the wagon were muddied and broken, some of it damaged beyond recognition. A cast-iron stove, a floor-sweeper organdie dress, a hat from Kansas City, books and slates, and even the ancient, long-barrelled Winchester—the accumulations of almost thirty years of living—all gone. Lost, as most of her life had been lost, through plain female stubbornness.

Limp and bedraggled, Amilia Rathmore settled her thick-lensed spectacles on her nose and moved forlornly through the wreckage. Her fine china that she had clung to for so long and with such hardheaded determination. Gone. Broken bits and pieces sticking out of the mud, glistening like broken bones.

Well, she told herself grimly, she had nobody to blame but herself. She hadn't been *forced* to take part in this fool's mission. Nobody had *made* her travel nearly a hundred miles out of her way with a bungling cowhand, two murderers and, now, a hangman. It had been her notion from the start—an idiotic notion—and for no reason at all. No sensible reason. No reason that she wanted to think about.

But she thought about it anyway, just as she had continued to do things and think and say things that she would never have dreamed of doing or thinking or saying before . . . before meeting a lanky, homely cowhand, a nobody by the name of Jones.

Rupe Dobie watched as she picked through her ruined belongings, idly curious as to what she might be thinking, but not really interested. Nothing truly interested Rupe Dobie that didn't bear directly or indirectly on the fine old art of public neck-breaking.

Which brought up the matter of horses. There was work waiting for him in Fort Smith. To get to it, he had to have horses.

Looking in the rear of the wagon, he said, " What about it, Skoda? Them witch cards say where we ought to look for the horses?"

Levi brushed the hangman with a heavy-lidded gaze. " I didn't ask."

Unexpectedly, Dobie laughed. Bobby Jack Wilkes,

chained up front to the seat spring, turned and fixed the hangman with a look that was so cold and hate-filled that Dobie took an involuntary step backward.

"You see somethin' funny, hangman?"

Dobie squinted, wiping his loose mouth on his sleeve. When he had assured himself that the assassin's chances of breaking out of his chains and shackles were practically non-existent, he said, "Not exactly funny, Wilkes. Interestin', more like. Old Rupe Dobie, he always takes a personal interest, you might say, in gents like you that figure to dangle on my hangin' machine."

Bobby Jack's cat eyes flashed with the same wildness that he had shown the night before. But, at the sound of commotion, Kiowa Jones rose like some greenish ghost from a lump of mud-caked bedding. He looked straight into those queer cat eyes and said hoarsely, "I figure I still owe you somethin', Wilkes. I ain't so weak that I can't pay up, if that's the way you want it."

The assassin blinked, startled to see Jones rise so casually out of unconsciousness. Then he grinned with a peculiar savagery. "You're some fighter, Jones, when you got the other fellow in chains."

Kiowa returned the grin, with steel to spare. "You just remember that, Wilkes, and we'll get along fine." Feeling his neck, he raised himself to one elbow and spoke to the hangman. "Dobie, get to lookin' for the horses. If they pulled their stakes they probably drifted with the wind. Work the bottom, south of here, and the draws to the east."

With a surprised shrug the hangman nodded.

When Dobie was gone, Kiowa looked at Levi Skoda, and Levi answered the question before it was asked. "Miss Rathmore's all right, cowboy. A mite rattled, I guess, the storm and all. But there's good steel in her—she'll straighten up."

Kiowa sagged back on the bedding. He felt like an old, worn-out river, sluggish and silted up and not much use for anything or to anybody. He sighed and closed his eyes and went to sleep almost instantly.

The next time he opened his eyes it was midday. He

squinted at Skoda, glared angrily at Bobby Jack Wilkes, then raised himself and bawled, "Miss Rathmore, why ain't we on the road?"

Amilia Rathmore looked in the back of the wagon. "I didn't think you were in any condition to travel."

Kiowa snorted. "Down in south Texas cowhands get this buggered-up in a light day of brush-poppin'. Did Dobie round up the horses?"

She nodded. "My team, and the bay you've been riding, but not the grey."

Kiowa grinned toothily at Bobby Jack. "Looks like you'll be ridin' indoors the rest of the way to Fort Smith," he said sourly.

The assassin glared darkly and killed Kiowa a hundred times in his thoughts. Amilia Rathmore raised a surprised eyebrow. "If you're sure you're up to travelling, I'll get Mr. Dobie to bring up the team."

Levi Skoda, oblivious to all else, continued laying out the soggy cards.

They rattled that day over the heavy prairie and through patches of cross timber that were all but impassable, as shabby and bedraggled as a family of droughted-out nesters. Which, Kiowa decided, might not be a bad thing to look like, at that.

On Kiowa's direction they bore due east, staying shy of the river, veering south of South Canadian and dodging all other settlements that lay along the north-south diagonal of the Katy right of way. Toward sundown they jolted across the twin steel tracks somewhere to the north of Krebs, a settlement of Italian coal miners, and made camp on a heavily wooded creek.

Kiowa managed to drag himself out of the wagon and sit before the fire while Amilia Rathmore started supper. He felt as weak as buttermilk, and his neck was as stiff as the butt end of a loaded quirt. But at least he was alive. Thanks again to a female schoolteacher.

Rupe Dobie, looking like a muddy, storm-frazzled scarecrow, hunkered near the fire and gazed professionally at Kiowa's neck. "Nothin' personal," he said pleasantly, "but, professionally speakin', I'm mighty relieved it wasn't Mr. Wilkes that got hisself shot in the neck that way. Man with that kind of wound makes a clean hangin' next to impossible."

"And you do enjoy a good, clean hangin'," Kiowa muttered with heavy sarcasm.

The hangman smiled loosely. "Every man to his own work, I say. I like to do a good job, like anybody else."

On a weak and squeamish stomach, Kiowa turned the talk in another direction. "I've been wonderin'," he said, looking at Rupe Dobie's dark eyes. "Seems like you're roamin' around a long ways from your headquarters. What was you doin' over here in the Nations, anyhow?"

"Little matter of business, friend," the hangman said, not without a note of pride. "Public execution, down on the other side of Red River."

Kiowa stared. "You don't get enough of it in Fort Smith? You ride clear to Texas to get more?"

Rupe Dobie shook his head sadly. "That cuts me to the quick, friend. A hangman's a public servant, like a preacher, or a doctor. He goes where he's needed. Of course," he said thoughtfully, "there's the matter of money. I got to live, like anybody else, and hangin' pay's mighty little, friend, especially at a federal court like Fort Smith. It's a poor life, Jones, considerin' the trials a man like me has to endure." He spat forlornly into the fire. "You know of a place called Tycee, down below the Red?"

"I don't think so."

"County seat, but not much of a place, really. They was brothers to be hung—held up a road ranch and killed a stock tender, so the story had it. Anyhow, there they was, guilty as sin and everybody knowed it, but they was local boys and likeable enough when sober, and nobody at Tycee wanted to give them the drop. So the sheriff sent up to Fort Smith for Rupe Dobie." The hangman sat straighter and puffed out his chest. "Like I said, they was likeable boys, and I guess the folks wanted 'em to swing in style."

Sadly, the hangman ran a hand over his bald head. "It could of been a grand affair, friend. A grand affair. I done my best to get 'em to build a double gallows—it would of been a sight they'd talk about for years to come, in Tycee. But the sheriff wouldn't listen to it." He shrugged his shoulders resignedly.

Kiowa didn't want to hear any more, but he was caught in the grip of a powerful lethargy. The loss of blood had sapped his resistance. It was easier to sit still and say nothing than to order the hangman to keep his bloody experiences to himself.

Rupe Dobie drew a soggy plug of Battle Axe from his coat pocket and bit off a corner. "Let me tell you, friend," he said with feeling, "it ain't no easy thing bein' a public servant on an unenlightened frontier. Or, for the matter of that, anywhere."

Kiowa roused himself enough to say dryly, "You seem to be takin' it pretty good."

Dobie chewed thoughtfully and spat at the fire. "It's a job that's got to be done, that's the way I look at it. And there ain't many of us that's suited to the work. One thing, a hangman's got to have a good head for figures—I bet you never thought about that, did you? He's got to be able to look at a man, add up the strong points, take away the weak ones, and then figure the drop right down to a gnat's whisker. Take yourself, for inst——"

"Never mind," Kiowa growled.

Dobie assumed an injured air, then shrugged it off. "Yes, sir, friend," he said sombrely, "there's a sight more to hangin' than the gallows birds ever dream about. Like the time over in England—that's across the water—when they strung up a seagoin' badman by the name of Kidd. The first time they dropped him, the rope broke. They took him back to the scaffold and dropped him again. The rope broke *again*! Three times they had to make old Cap'n Kidd look up a rope, like they say, before it finally took. That's sorry workmanship, friend. I don't care where you find it. Never would of happened if old Rupe Dobie'd been there seein' to things."

"I bet," Kiowa said sourly.

Rupe turned a deaf ear to the sarcastic tone. "Of course," he droned, "there's worse on the frontier. Lots worse. It's a hard thing, I tell you, to see some poor devil of a horse thief pulled off the ground and left to dangle from a cottonwood limb until he finally checks in from strangulation. But that ain't hangin'. It's plain killin'."

Kiowa failed to see the difference, but maybe that was because of his weakened condition.

"There's plenty to be done," Rupe Dobie said, warming to his subject, "before an executioner can think about the actual drop. Take the rope—fine, hand-woven, five-strand Philippine abaca, and nothin' else. And the gallows—heavy oak, perfectly cured, so you don't have to worry about warpage that could cause the trap to stick. Or worse than that, cause the trap to bind and cause a slow drop, where the poor devil slides down the trap and dangles at the end of the rope and strangles. I hear there's executioners in foreign places that favour teakwood for buildin' a gallows, but give me honest oak every time. And well-oiled hinges on the trap, and a little grease on the bolt, so you can kick it loose without a fuss."

Kiowa grunted, wondering if Bobby Jack was getting this. And Levi Skoda. Letting himself be carried along with Rupe Dobie's enthusiasm, he could almost feel the touch of hemp on his throat, the hard lump of a hanging knot behind his ear.

"However," Dobie continued, "the important thing—the most important thing an executioner has to do—is to be able to size up a prisoner. A broke neck, snapped quick and clean, that's the thing to shoot at. Folks don't like to see the wretch kickin' and blubberin' at the end of a rope for maybe five, ten minutes, before he finally cashes in. But the worst thing that can happen, friend, is makin' a mistake in your drop, goin' the other direction. Give him two, three inches too much rope and . . ." Dobie clapped his hands sharply and Kiowa gave a startled grunt. "Just like that, friend! Yanks his head right off his shoulders. . . ."

Kiowa turned, looked at Dobie with glittering eyes. "Ain't it time you was lookin' after the horses?"

The hangman, about to answer in the negative, took a closer look at the cowhand's bearded face and changed his mind. "Maybe it is." He got to his feet and sidled away from the fire.

: : : :

After a supper of boiled beans and dry-salt and some canned tomatoes that had been salvaged from the storm, Kiowa huddled close to the fire, greedily soaking up the warmth. He roused himself enough to direct Dobie's handling of the horses and prisoners, then he returned to his cross-legged, statue-like watch by the fire, trying to warm his bones, like some shrivelled old Plains Apache preparing himself for the dying grounds.

"Mr. Jones."

Kiowa raised his head, squinting, surprised to see that it was almost dark. The low, rolling hills, crosslighted by the dying sun, bristled with scrub timber. For a moment the scene stood out boldly in stark relief, like sun-dance scars on the chest of some grizzled old Cheyenne warrior. Then it was gone—a scene wiped from the face of a black slate.

"You want somethin', Miss Rathmore?"

"Don't you think you ought to rest, Mr. Jones?"

"I'm restin' fine. Much obliged, just the same."

"Perhaps I ought to dress that wound again."

"The wound's been dressed, Miss Rathmore. It's a straight, clean furrow with a good scab. No proud flesh, no trouble at all, except that it hurts right down to my knees. But that's to be expected."

He told her nothing that she didn't already know. The wound was painful but superficial, and with a little care and attention his strength would soon return. It wasn't the wound that she wanted to talk about, and both of them knew it. A disturbing possibility crossed Kiowa's mind.

"Maybe you've got it in your head to pull out?" he suggested. "Well"—he shrugged—"I couldn't blame you if you did. The goin' hasn't been easy, and there's not much chance it'll improve between here and Fort Smith. But I've been doin' some thinkin', about that bounty. You've been out a good deal of money, in the way of time and lost supplies—so that bounty's yours, Miss Rathmore, if you'll give me the loan of your team and wagon. You don't have to come along yourself, if you don't want to. I can take you back to one of the Katy stops and you can catch the cars on to Tahlequah. . . ."

She peered down at him, not angrily, but with a good deal of impatience. "You are bound and determined not to take that money for yourself, aren't you?"

"Well, like I said—"

"I know what you said," she told him crisply. "But I don't believe it. Money—a large amount of money—is not to be considered lightly. Wealth means responsibility, and that's the thing you are afraid of, isn't it, Mr. Jones?"

"Maybe," Kiowa said coolly.

"What, exactly, do you have against responsibility, Mr. Jones?"

"Well," Kiowa said uncomfortably, "nothin', I guess. Long's it belongs to somebody else." He grinned feebly.

She frowned and made an impatient gesture with her hand. "Don't be flip, Mr. Jones. I want to know. Perhaps I have a right to know, considering what we've been through together these past few days."

Kiowa probed his groggy mind but could think of no answer that wouldn't make him seem foolish.

"Haven't you ever thought of getting married?" Amilia Rathmore asked bluntly. "And have a home, a family, like other men?"

A lump of suspicion rose in Kiowa's throat. "A cowhand can't afford them things."

"A cowhand with that bounty money in the bank could afford them."

"I think," Kiowa said lamely, "I better get some rest, after all."

Amilia Rathmore snorted, turned on her heel and began cleaning what the storm had left of her dishes.

CHAPTER TWELVE

A MOODY SILENCE settled over the wagon as the team battered its way through heavy stands of scrub oak and scattered hickory, the Cross Timbers. It was heavy going, but safe, Kiowa figured. Even the outlaws steered shy of the Cross Timbers.

Kiowa's strength returned slowly but steadily, and he saddled the sturdy little bay quarter horse and scouted ahead and to either side of the wagon, looking for the best passages through the brush. He changed their course from due east to north-east, heading generally toward the plateau country where the Arkansas forked with the Canadian.

Late that afternoon Kiowa returned from a scout to report a thinning of the brush and a passable camp site not far ahead. He climbed out of the saddle and mounted the wagon seat beside Amilia Rathmore, glad enough for the chance to rest.

Miss Rathmore nodded ahead to a sparsely covered ridge. "Did you ride as far as that high ground?"

Kiowa, knowing what was on her mind, said, "No need to worry about somebody pickin' up our trail. Not in this brush." He took the lines and they rode on for a while in silence.

Then, in her abrupt way, "Did you mean what you said yesterday, Mr. Jones? About seeing the prisoners to Fort Smith yourself?"

Kiowa hunched his shoulders in vague discomfort. He had said it, and he had meant it, at the time. Maybe he still did, but he didn't like being prodded into a thing, like a balky steer being poled into a cattle car.

She asked again, "Did you mean it, Mr. Jones?"

"I said it, didn't I?"

"And still you intend to turn down that bounty money?"

Kiowa ground his teeth and turned a beseeching face toward heaven. Amilia Rathmore wisely let the subject rest.

Bobby Jack Wilkes began to complain that his chains were binding. Levi Skoda peevishly demanded water and a fresh winding on his leg. Rupe Dobie was even more syrupy and obnoxious and sadistic than usual. The long trip was beginning to tell on all of them, honing razorlike edges to their tempers.

Amilia Rathmore, womanlike, was loath to let a question run loose and unanswered. "Why," she asked after a long pause, "did you decide to go on to Fort Smith? What made you?"

"Nothin' *made* me," Kiowa answered shortly. "I just decided. Maybe because I don't like bein' shot. What difference does it make?"

"More than you might imagine," she said in the cool, lecturing tone of a schoolteacher. Then she smiled in a way that was particularly maddening and said, "But never mind. You've answered my question."

He glared. "I have?"

"The matter of responsibility that we talked about. You're learning to accept it, Mr. Jones, though you probably don't realize it yet. You began to accept it the moment you took charge of that dead marshal's prisoners."

Kiowa snarled, "You're loco!"

But she only gazed straight ahead and smiled placidly.

"Loco," Kiowa muttered again, to himself.

Bobby Jack Wilkes, in that cocky tone that grated like flint dust on Kiowa's nerves, said, "Looks like we'll be in for a little company, cowboy."

Kiowa turned suddenly and pain tightened around his neck like a noose. Then he saw them, four horsemen on their back trail, the animals high-stepping through the tangle of brush and scrub oak. The wagon topped a small rise and they got a brief, clear glimpse at the trailing riders. Rifles on their saddles. Always a bad sign, when you're on the lookout for trouble.

"Friends of yours, cowboy?" the assassin taunted.

"Shut up," Kiowa said coldly. He cracked the lines over the backs of the team and edged the wagon off the crest of the ridge and moved cautiously along the far side.

Amilia Rathmore took his arm. "What do you think?"

"Travellers, most likely."

"In the Cross Timbers?"

Kiowa grinned sourly to himself. They weren't travellers. They were men on a mission, and there wasn't much doubt that they were following the wagon.

Rupe Dobie edged up from the rear of the wagon and Kiowa could feel the hangman's sticky breath on the back of his neck. "What about it, Jones?" he asked nervously. "You figure it's a posse?"

Kiowa shrugged, his eyes fixed on the trackless slope ahead. "What you aim to do," the hangman demanded, "if they're bounty hunters come lookin' for Wilkes?"

Kiowa turned and grinned savagely in Rupe Dobie's face. "A little patience, hangman. We'll know what to do when we know what the horsebackers're up to." Kiowa shot a look at the sun, which lazed over the western ridges. Less than an hour high. He forgot about the camp site that he had picked out and decided to make for the high ground. If the riders were what they seemed to be, he wanted to be in a position to fight back when they made their move.

"Make for the ridge," he told Amilia Rathmore, handing her the lines, "there's some things I got to do."

He began emptying the Winchester for a thorough inspection and cleaning. A dirty rifle had saved his life once, when it had been in Bobby Jack's hands, but the next time Kiowa meant to hang on to it himself. Miss Rathmore watched as he cleaned the cartridges, ran patches through the barrel and cleaned what he could reach of the action. "And don't try to call it acceptin' responsibility," he said dryly, reading her thoughts. "I just don't want to break the habit of livin'."

She smiled in that peculiar way that was beginning to be as irritating as her spoken opinions.

Muttering, Kiowa finished with his own rifle, took up Amilia Rathmore's vintage Winchester and checked it carefully. When he had finished with the two rifles and the revolver, he glanced back at Rupe Dobie. "You know anything about guns?"

The hangman shrugged. "Like anybody else."

Kiowa handed him the revolver. "Keep a watch on our backtrail. Don't let the horsebackers get too close until we know who they are."

Bobby Jack laughed softly. "It's a long, long way to Fort Smith, cowboy, and you ain't never goin' to make it."

Kiowa shot him a flint-tipped look. "If I don't make it, you don't make it. That's a promise I just made myself."

The assassin's laughter trailed off to an uneasy silence. He didn't like this new, quiet toughness that was beginning to show itself in the cowhand's actions and speech.

The wagon jolted over the sandstone spine of the ridge, and Kiowa decided this would be as good a place as any for seeing out the night. The horsemen had fallen back out of sight, lost somewhere in the bristling scrub timber. "Everybody stay in the wagon." Kiowa got down and scouted the surrounding area on the bay, but the horsebackers were either laying back or had taken another trail. And Kiowa didn't think they had taken another trail.

When he got back to the wagon, the nervous hangman said, "Who are they? Did you see them?"

"I didn't see nothin' but twenty miles of scrub oak spread out in all directions. But we'll hear from 'em come nightfall, I figure, if they're bounty hunters."

Amilia Rathmore asked wearily, "Are you sure they're bounty hunters, Mr. Jones?"

"No. But men don't travel the Cross Timbers without they've got a good reason."

"How could they know who we are?" Rupe Dobie fretted. "With both prisoners here in the wagon, under canvas, how could they know?"

Kiowa shrugged. "Maybe they're suspicious as we are, of travellers in the Cross Timbers." He climbed down from the saddle and began unhitching the team and stripping the bay. No matter what was to come later, the horses had to be seen to—a little water from the wagon supply, a handful of grain and stake them out in the new grass that grew between the clusters of stunted trees.

"Ought I make a fire?" Amilia Rathmore asked.

"No. Stay in the wagon, you and Dobie, but keep the guns out of sight till they're needed." Far off to the west Kiowa caught the faint sound of a nervous horse pawing the hard earth. There went the hope that the horsemen hadn't been following the wagon. Kiowa grabbed his rifle and made his way back to the crest of the ridge, peering over the sandstone outcropping.

Somebody was down there, all right—a big man in cattleman's garb, hunkering down in the dappled shade. Kiowa studied the figure over the barrel of the rifle, wondering where the other three had got to.

A voice over to the left of the big man, and farther up the slope, called quietly, "Here it is. I see where they crossed the ridge."

The big man stood up, pushed his hat back on his forehead and strode into the open. "Huck, can you see the wagon?"

"Not yet. Makin' dry camp, most likely, on the far slope."

"You see anything of the horses?" the big man asked.

"Don't see 'em yet. But we're gettin' close."

The big man took off his hat and wiped his forehead on his sleeve. He was a young man, in his early thirties, but there was only a fringe of sandy hair behind his ears. The top of his head was as bald as a glass egg. "Huck, can you see anything of Moonlight and Oren?"

"Over here, Jim," a voice called from the big man's right. "We seen one jasper stakin' out the team and the bay. No sign of the geldin', though."

The big man, the one called Jim, stood a little straighter, grew a little bigger and angrier as he cradled a silver-mounted shotgun in the crook of his arm. "There ain't no use puttin' it off," he said tonelessly. "Close in on the wagon, now, before dark comes."

Kiowa couldn't see the men referred to as Huck, Moonlight and Oren, but the boss of the party was the big bald-headed gent with the fancy scatter-gun. There wasn't any doubt about that. Jim whatever-his-name-was, in a purposeful crouch, started up the slope to join the others. Kiowa, squinting over the sights of his rifle, wondered if bounty hunters were like Indians. Shoot the chief and the others would scatter. He caressed the Winchester's trigger but made no move to squeeze it. Killing, he had learned, he could do, if he had to, but not killing in cold blood. Anyhow, Indians and bounty hunters were different brands of poison.

Then:

" Drop the saddle gun, cowboy." The voice purred, almost whispered, a short distance from Kiowa's left ear.

Kiowa jumped, startled, and almost jerked the trigger by accident. He turned his head, careless of his stiff and aching neck, and winced involuntarily. A thick, blunt man with flashing eyes and a beard as black as line-camp coffee, stepped in quickly with a long-barrelled Colt Cavalry revolver and cracked the blue steel across Kiowa's forearm.

Kiowa dropped his rifle without knowing it, then, as if from a great distance, heard the weapon clattering on the rocky ground. The Winchester that he had so carefully cleaned just a few minutes before. Kiowa fell back a step, his mouth cottony. The bearded man casually aimed directly between Kiowa's eyes, the muzzle inches from Kiowa's head.

" You ought to of dropped the saddle gun when I told you," the man said gravely. " I didn't break that arm for you, did I?"

Kiowa swallowed with difficulty. ". . . I don't think so," he managed, working his fingers, flexing the knotted muscle.

" That your outfit on the other side of the hump?"

With an emptiness where his gut ought to be, Kiowa nodded. The man grinned faintly, but the expression was lost in the wilderness of black beard.

" Call your boys in, Jim. I think we've got our man."

Kiowa blinked, then frowned, puzzled. He pulled his gaze away from the hypnotic muzzle of the Cavalry revolver and searched its owner's dark eyes. " What do you mean, you ' got your man '? Who do you think I am?"

The bearded man shrugged. " Your name? That don't matter. But if you're a horse thief, that does matter and it looks like that's what you are. Or maybe you can explain how you come to have Jim Aldridge's favourite quarter horse staked out below your wagon?"

It was then that Kiowa settled down enough to notice the hard-worn sheriff's badge pinned to the bearded man's blue serge vest. Kiowa stared at the badge and felt limp with relief. "Mister, you gave me a bad turn. Are you really a sheriff?"

"Able Moonlight, Addison County, Texas."

"You're a little off your reservation, ain't you, Sheriff?"

"For a man that steals horses—especially Jim Aldridge's horses—there ain't no boundary he can jump over and play safe."

"You got this all wrong, Sheriff. I ain't no horse thief."

"You better tell that to Jim," Sheriff Moonlight said placidly. "He's the big bald-headed gent comin' up the slope."

Kiowa's sensation of relief was beginning to sour. "If you'll just listen, Sheriff. I can explain about that horse."

"I hope you can. For your sake." Carefully, he parted his beard and spat tobacco juice into the brush. "I never was a man to stand still for lynchin'. But the way Jim and the boys're worked up . . ."

He left the thought hanging, dangerously. Then Jim Aldridge, his eyes blazing, bore down on them. The big man snarled, and before Kiowa could raise a hand in defence, Aldridge had caught him over the left ear with the twin barrels of the shotgun.

Kiowa didn't remember going down,only looking up at the darkening sky where pain flashes danced like summer lightning. Four faces looked down at him, two grinning, one in anger and Sheriff Moonlight's with no expression at all. Groggily, Kiowa started to get up, but boot heels tramped on his arms, pinning him to the ground.

"Huck, what did you do with the rope?" Aldridge demanded.

A long, strung-out cowhand with brick-red hair and trail beard grinned at his boss. "Left it on the ridge, Mr. Aldridge, but everything's ready to go. Slipknot's already tied."

Huck was one of the men who had a boot heel on Kiowa's arm. The other one, the one Aldridge had called Oren, was a small, wiry man with the barrel-stave legs of a bronc peeler. He had a pinched face, wrinkled like a Concord raisin and about the same colour. At a silent signal from their boss, Huck and Oren stepped back and allowed Kiowa to rise to his knees.

"What'd you do with the geldin'?" the bald Aldridge demanded.

Kiowa, on all fours, swayed and shook his pounding head. "What geldin'?"

With cold savagery, the big man stepped in and slammed a sharp-toed boot into Kiowa's ribs. Kiowa went sprawling on his back again, gasping for breath.

"Don't talk smart to Jim Aldridge, horse thief. We already seen you stake out the bay. What'd you do with the grey geldin'?"

It got through slowly, a little at a time, what horse they were talking about. "The grey run off," Kiowa panted, prodding his ribs tenderly before he rolled over and crawled back to his knees. "Durin' the storm. He was tied to the wagon, the wagon blowed over and the horse got away. But I can tell you how I got them horses, if you'll just——"

Aldridge said coldly to his red-headed hand, "Huck, fetch the rope. And look for a tree big enough to hang this horse thief."

"Listen, Aldridge, I didn't steal them horses!"

"If you can't find a tree big enough," Aldridge went on, ignoring the interruption, "we'll have to drag him. And that's never a very pretty sight."

Kiowa realized that sweat had plastered his shirt to his back, although a chilled wind was sifting through the stunted trees. In his great rush to present a persuasive explanation, the words stuck in his throat and he couldn't make a sound.

Huck jogged off through the brush and in a few minutes came back with a coiled lariat over his shoulder. Kiowa stared dumbly at the common slipknot that the cowhand was shaking out.

"You find a tree?" the bald man asked.

"There's a hickory that might do," Huck told him. "But it's over on the far slope, not far from the wagon."

"Anybody in the wagon?"

Huck shrugged, then, with an expert flip, dropped the loop over Kiowa's head and pulled it tight. Kiowa yelped when the rough hemp sawed against the bullet wound.

Jim Aldridge stood spread-eagled, hands gripping the scatter-gun, towering giant-like over the others as he glared down at the man he meant to hang. "I've been on your trail almost two weeks, horse thief," he growled. "Nobody steals horses from Jim Aldridge and lives to brag about it. Nobody. You understand?"

The meaning was clear. There was nothing subtle about Jim Aldridge. Staving off panic, Kiowa worked his mouth, but the rope choked off his words.

"Loosen the rope," Aldridge said coldly, "maybe he wants to tell the truth about the geldin'."

Grudgingly, Huck loosened the rope enough to allow speech. "I'm tellin' you the truth, Aldridge, or whatever your name is. Some bounty hunters jumped us back in the Chickasaw Nation, tried to take my prisoners, so I had to shoot 'em. I can show you the graves. One was young and green and went by the name of Jelly. The other one was older and smarter—the young one called him Morgan. Morgan was ridin' the bay, Jelly was on the grey geldin'. When my own animal was killed . . ." He made a helpless gesture. "Well, I guess I just kind of borrowed the horses the two scalpers was ridin'."

The sheriff, Aldridge and the two hands shot curious glances all around.

"Morgan and Jelly?" the sheriff asked.

"That's what they called each other. You know 'em?"

A long minute passed before anyone made a sound. At last Jim Aldridge said flatly, "They used to work for me. But they was no-account. I fired 'em two weeks ago, maybe a little longer."

Once more the dizzy sensation of relief made itself felt. "There you are," Kiowa said, reaching for the noose about his neck. "They was sore because you fired them, so they figured to get even by stealin' a couple of your saddle horses. How was I to know they was horse thieves?"

The sheriff stroked his black beard and looked thoughtful. "There might be somethin' in what he says, Jim."

"He's lyin'," Aldridge snarled. "I don't aim to be quick-talked out of a hangin'."

Able Moonlight gazed unconcernedly at Kiowa's injured neck. "You said bounty hunters, stranger. Jelly and Morgan was kind of wild and no-account, but I never heard they was bounty hunters."

Cautiously, Kiowa loosened the knot at his throat. "They was when I met up with them. Look . . ." He tried to sound reasonable and convincing. Aldridge, in spite of his hot temper, was just an ordinary cowman, and Kiowa was convinced that, if he could just find the right words, he could still work himself out of this trouble. "Look, I know how you feel about the horses. But things ain't the way they look. Give me a few minutes to set you straight, and you'll be able to see I'm tellin' the truth."

"I already had my fill of chin music, mister." The big cattleman nodded to Huck, indicating that he was ready to get on with the business at hand.

Huck jerked on the rope. "Get on your feet, cowboy. Or do you want us to drag you over the ridge to the hangin' tree?"

"Hold on a minute," Sheriff Moonlight said mildly, almost idly, as he parted his black beard and took a big bite of chewin'. "Don't seem like too much to ask, Jim. If the stranger's got a story, maybe it wouldn't do no harm if we give him a listen."

Aldridge's eyes flashed. But behind the sheriff's off-handed tone there was something else, a concealed toughness, like a fighting knife in a velvet sheath. Kiowa heard it, or sensed it, and so did the big rancher and his two hands. For a moment Aldridge's gaze locked with Moonlight's, and it was the rancher who looked away.

"All right!" Grudgingly, angrily. "All right, but talk fast, mister. I don't aim to put this business off much longer."

There was only one way to tell his story, and that was

from the beginning. Moonlight scowled, and Aldridge looked his anger and impatience as Kiowa doubled back in time and space, back to the day that he had happened on to the dying marshal and the prisoners. Sheriff Moonlight's dark eyes glittered at the mention of Bobby Jack Wilkes.

"That the pay killer with the big bounty on his head?"

"A thousand dollars," Kiowa said. "That's the legal one. Wilkes would double it, out of his own pocket, to the man that breaks him free before we get to Fort Smith."

The red-headed cowhand made a sound of surprise. The one called Oren rubbed his chin and looked thoughtful—and greedy.

"Two thousand dollars! That would buy a whole herd of grey geldin's, Mr. Aldridge."

"I ain't lookin' for a herd," the rancher said grimly. "Just my own stock."

Kiowa went on with the story. "These two hands of yours, Jelly and Morgan, I guess they picked up news of the bounty while ridin' the high line. So they tracked us down and made their play . . . and got theirselves killed, the way it turned out. And that's how I come to have your horses," he said, looking at the big rancher.

Moonlight and Aldridge swapped guarded glances. "You got that hot-shot killer in the wagon now, you say?" the sheriff asked.

Kiowa nodded. "Him, and a bohunk by the name of Skoda, and the female schoolteacher that owns the wagon—Miss Amilia Rathmore." Then, as an afterthought, "And one more passenger—a gent that you might've heard about, Sheriff. Rupe Dobie."

The sheriff's bushy eyebrows shot up in disbelief. "The Fort Smith hangman?"

"That's the one. Been doin' a little rope work down in your territory, he claims, and was headin' back for Arkansas when his mule went down. He's been ridin' in our wagon ever since."

"Maybe we better have a look at that wagon," Moonlight said, looking at Aldridge. "As humans go, Rupe Dobie don't come very high, but I don't reckon he'd have any reason to lie for this stranger and risk gettin' hisself in trouble with the law."

Aldridge backed down a little, but grudgingly. "You're the sheriff, Able. But you better know what you're doin'."

Moonlight elected to overlook the rancher's thinly veiled threat. Aldridge, with an angry jerk of his chin, sent Oren into the brush to round up their horses. Huck kept the rope taut, the noose drawn around Kiowa's neck. He grinned widely, enjoying the discomfort in Kiowa's face.

"You better be spinnin' a straight yarn, cowboy. Mr. Aldridge ain't hardly in no mood to get talked out of a hangin'."

"Shut up, Huck," the rancher said tonelessly. "After the sheriff satisfies himself that we've got the right man, there's still time to deal with this horse thief."

Oren came up with the horses. The possemen mounted and headed toward the ridge, Kiowa stumbling after them, jogging awkwardly to keep the rough rope from sawing at his neck. When they reached the ridge, Sheriff Moonlight motioned for Huck to bring Kiowa forward. "You hear me good, cowboy," Moonlight said, those dark eyes boring into Kiowa's skull. "Call down to the wagon. Tell the woman to get out. Have the hangman peel back the sheet—I want to see everything you're carryin', especially the guns. I want to see the guns on the ground. You got that straight?"

Kiowa twisted his neck to get breathing space. "You're an easy man to understand, Sheriff. I got it straight."

"There's another thing," Jim Aldridge said coldly. "If everything don't go just like Able says, I give Huck the nod and he'll drag you clear to the Kansas line. There won't be enough of you left to bait a wolf trap with."

Sheriff Moonlight gazed into the greying distance and chewed placidly on his cud of tobacco.

As Kiowa topped the ridge at the end of Huck's rope he wondered hollowly what he could say or do, without getting himself shot or dragged, to indicate to Rupe Dobie that a wrong word from him would mean a sudden and probably painful death for Kiowa Jones. It wasn't a comforting notion, placing his life in the hands of a professional hangman. Especially when Dobie didn't know what any of this was about, or what was expected of him. But Rupe was a duly appointed officer of a federal court, and for that reason Moonlight might be willing to take the hangman's word for Kiowa's innocence.

There was one serious hitch. The possemen had the notion that Dobie—if there was anything to Kiowa's story in the first place—had been travelling with them at the time of the fight with Jelly and Morgan. They were expecting a first-hand account of the fight in which Kiowa had acquired the stolen horses. Kiowa didn't like to speculate on what would happen when they learned that Dobie had joined the party later and was not a first-hand witness after all.

CHAPTER THIRTEEN

AMILIA RATHMORE, peering over the sights of her newly cleaned rifle, breathed in sharply when she saw Kiowa Jones topping the ridge. Rupe Dobie, grasping Kiowa's revolver in both hands, also made a sound of surprise.

"Somethin's wrong. I don't like the look of this, Miss Rathmore."

In the failing light they couldn't see the noose about Kiowa's neck until the red-headed cowhand rode into view holding the other end of the rope. Bobby Jack Wilkes, hunching against the side of the wagon box, worked the canvas up enough to glimpse Kiowa and the four riders on the spiny ridge. The assassin threw his head back and laughed with glee.

"There you are," he gurgled. "Didn't I tell him he'd never get me to Fort Smith?"

"Maybe . . ." Rupe Dobie swallowed nervously. "Maybe they ain't bounty hunters at all. You don't know everything, Wilkes."

Bobby Jack laughed again. "I know a tight fit when I see one. Look at the noose around Jones's neck. You think them gents just kind of mistook him for a maverick yearlin'?"

With deliberate movements, Amilia Rathmore drew her rifle into the wagon and said coldly, "That will be quite enough, Mr. Wilkes."

The beginning of a sneer showed at the corners of the assassin's mouth. Then, on second thought, he merely grinned and shrugged his shoulders. Miss Rathmore's face was bone-white, expressionless, as she turned her attention back to the ridge, watching through a crack between the lifted canvas and the wagon box. Then Kiowa's voice floated down the brush-strewn slope.

"Dobie. Miss Rathmore. These gents ain't bounty hunters, but there's kind of a mix-up . . ."

Miss Rathmore saw the big man who seemed to be the leader threaten Kiowa with his saddle gun. Kiowa moved his shoulders, then called again, his voice distant and emotionless. "Just listen to me and do what I tell you and everything will be all right. Miss Rathmore, climb out of the wagon, stand where we can see you and put your gun on the ground. Dobie, untie the wagon sheet and peel it back . . ."

At another threatening gesture from the big horseman, Kiowa's words trailed off. Something happened to Amilia Rathmore's face. The toughness was no longer there. The fight had gone out of her. She was frightened and numb.

Levi Skoda spoke quietly, with an almost feminine gentleness. "I think you better do like he says, Miss Rathmore. Maybe they ain't bounty hunters. Maybe it's some kind of mistake."

Wilkes snorted. "A mistake, all right, hunky. When that cowhand decided to take on a marshal's job, that's when he made his mistake."

But Amilia Rathmore seemed to draw strength from Skoda's hint of encouragement. "What makes you think it might be a mistake, Mr. Skoda?"

Skoda looked away and studied his chained wrists in discomfort. Bobby Jack Wilkes sensed the truth and prodded him gleefully. "The lady asked you a question, hunky. How come you think they ain't bounty hunters? You see it in them hoodoo cards of yours?"

Levi shrugged his slight shoulders.

"There you are, ma'am," the assassin said sarcastically. "Jones ain't got a thing to worry about. The hunky's hoodoo cards has told him all about it."

Fever spots burned in Skoda's face but he said nothing. Miss Rathmore, with the submerged terror returning, said tightly, "I don't suppose we have a choice. Mr. Dobie, please untie the wagon sheet and work it forward."

: : : :

The rope was drawing steadily tighter about Kiowa's throat, and it was with relief that he saw Miss Rathmore climbing down from the wagon. Then the wagon sheet fluttered loosely as the hangman began working it back over the bows.

Jim Aldridge scowled as he looked down into the clutter of the wagon box. Able Moonlight chewed thoughtfully. "Just like the stranger said, Jim. That's Dobie, all right——I'd know that buzzard's face a mile away. And there's the woman. And the two prisoners, shackled hand and foot, just like he said."

"Maybe," Aldridge admitted grudgingly. "But I still want to hear the hangman's side of it."

The sheriff hitched in his saddle and spat over his horse's neck. "Whatever you say. We might as well get started."

Miss Rathmore and Rupe Dobie stood woodenly beside the wagon, their weapons on the ground in front of them, as Kiowa stumbled down the slope, followed by the four horse-backers.

The possemen reined up a short piece from the wagon, and Kiowa came to an abrupt halt as the rope yanked at his raw neck. He looked at Amilia Rathmore's drawn face, but only in passing, as his gaze moved on to the hangman. Dobie was nervous, and that was bad. Kiowa looked steadily into those shifting eyes and thought: Back me up, Dobie, and maybe we'll all get out of this with our hides on.

Aldridge shot an uninterested glance at Amilia Rathmore, then aimed his attention at Rupe Dobie. "I hear you're the hangman over at Fort Smith."

Dobie swallowed the rising lump in his throat and nodded.

"Talk up, man. My patience's pullin' at the end of its rope."

The hangman spoke with considerable effort. "I'm an officer of the court, deputy marshal in charge of executions."

The red-headed cowhand hooted laughter. His side-kick, Oren, grinned, but Kiowa noticed that Oren seemed more interested in the prisoners in the wagon than in the hangman or the stolen horses.

"All right, hangerman," the big rancher snarled. "Tell me about my animals. The bay quarter horse, and the grey geldin'. I want to hear just how this horse thief"—indicating Kiowa—"managed to steal them."

Rupe Dobie swallowed again, his eyes darting from face to face like dark bees in a locust grove. At last, with a strong attempt at dignity, he drew himself up and said, "I can't tell you how the horses was stolen, mister . . ."

Kiowa sagged hopelessly. Then, with one last effort, he caught the hangman's nervous gaze and held it, and somehow made Dobie feel the urgency and the anger that was in him.

"Go on," Jim Aldridge said ominously. "Why can't you tell me about my stolen horses, hangerman?"

Dobie shuffled uncomfortably and drew the back of his hand over his mouth. "Well . . . for one thing I wasn't there." Those eyes darting from Kiowa to the rancher. "I wasn't even acquainted with the two bounty hunters, the ones called Morgan and Jelly."

Kiowa frowned in surprise, and so did Aldridge. "I ain't talkin' about Morgan and Jelly," the big rancher said coldly. "I'm talkin' about the man that stole my animals."

For good or bad, the hangman had found his direction and knew where he was going. A new look, a look of confidence, settled on Dobie's homely features, and even the tone of his voice was steady and unruffled. Kiowa held his breath.

"And so am I talkin' about the man—the men—that stole your animals, Mr. . . ."

Aldridge wanted to ignore the gap of silence that asked his name, but Rupe Dobie outwaited him. "Aldridge," he muttered. "Jim Aldridge."

"Mr. Aldridge," the hangman went on with controlled calm. "Like I said, I wasn't there when Morgan and Jelly stole your horses, so how could I tell you about it?"

The rancher's eyes blazed. But Dobie rushed on, almost as though he knew that this sudden burst of courage wasn't going to last for ever. "The bounty hunters had the horses, Mr. Aldridge. Mr. Jones had no way of knowin' they was stolen from you. And he couldn't just turn them loose on the prairie, fully saddled and bitted, could he?" Now that he had hit his stride, the hangman was beginning to enjoy the sound of his own voice. "So Mr. Jones did what any honest, law-abidin' man would of done, Aldridge; he caught your animals and was takin' them to Fort Smith to turn over to the legal authority——"

Aldridge cut in harshly. "Did you see this, hangerman, with your own eyes? Did you see Morgan and Jelly on my horses?"

"I did," Dobie said without batting an eye. "You have my word for it, the word of a federal court officer. You wouldn't want me to take word back to Fort Smith, would you, that Jim Aldridge interfered with a government officer in the performance of his duty?"

Aldridge, for the first time, didn't seem quite so sure of his own power. "What do you mean?"

"Mr. Jones—the man you were about to lynch—is an official officer of the Fort Smith court. Do you know what the penalty is, Mr. Aldridge, for criminal assault on a federal officer?"

The rancher shot a guarded glance at Able Moonlight, but the bearded sheriff was gazing into the far distance with great unconcern. "Well, Sheriff!" Aldridge demanded angrily.

Moonlight roused himself enough to spit, then look thoughtfully at the rancher. "Jim, the penalty for assaultin' a federal officer runs about five years in the Leavenworth prison, near as I can recall . . ."

"That ain't what I mean!" Aldridge exploded. "Do you

believe his story? Do you think Morgan and Jelly are the ones that stole my horses?"

"I believe it," Moonlight said mildly. "What's more, I believe you ought to back away from this thing and head back for home range . . . after apologizin' to these good people, of course."

The rancher's weathered face burned scarlet. He rose in his saddle, glaring at the sheriff, his shoulders tensed, and for a moment it looked as though he might turn his threatening gun on Moonlight as he had on Kiowa. But when they locked angry glances, it was the big rancher who was the first to break it off.

"Oren," Aldridge said through clenched teeth, "ride down and pull the bay's stake pin. We're takin' him home."

The wry-faced little hand ducked his head, then kneed around the wagon and headed toward the lower end of the slope where Kiowa had staked the animals.

"I won't be satisfied with gettin' back just one of my animals," Aldridge announced grimly to all concerned. "I hold you responsible, mister." He glared at Kiowa. "How long has the geldin' been gone, and which way did he head?"

Kiowa, pushing his fingers between his throat and the rope, slipped the knot and worked the noose over his head. When Aldridge failed to react, when the red-headed hand let the rope lie where Kiowa had dropped it and then slowly began to reel it in, Kiowa knew that the danger of the moment was over. Perversely, that was when his knees started knocking. Somewhere inside himself he began to shake, and he couldn't stop. He was surprised to hear his own voice cool and steady, as he told the possemen about the storm, about how the wagon had gone over and the grey gelding had broken loose and bolted, probably to the south, along the stream where they had camped.

"Huck, when Oren comes back with the bay, I want the two of you to ride back to that creek. Travel downstream till you find the geldin'. Me and the sheriff will start back to headquarters." He paused, gazing levelly at the hand. "You and Oren come back with that grey, or don't come back at all. You understand?"

Huck grinned self-consciously. " We'll come back with the grey, Mr. Aldridge."

From the wagon, Bobby Jack Wilkes had watched the scene in dumb disbelief. He had been so sure that the horse-backers had come to set him free and collect the double bounty. He couldn't believe that all this commotion could be over a pair of horses. He kept waiting, the time grating on his nerves like a bone saw, waiting for the possemen to show their real hand and let him go. At last, with bitter reluctance, he was forced to accept the truth.

Levi Skoda, in a kind of stony amusement, watched the wildness grow in the assassin's eyes. "You oughtn't to of laughed at the tarot, Wilkes. It's always a mistake to show disrespect for the cards."

With a wolfish snarl, Bobby Jack lunged at the quietly smiling hunky, lunged so savagely that his shoulders snapped painfully as he came to the end of his chains. Then, with a characteristic force of will, he blotted Levi Skoda from his mind and yelled at the horsebackers, clanging his chains against the wagon bed for attention.

" Listen to me! All of you! I'm Bobby Jack Wilkes and there's a thousand dollars' bounty on my head to the man that gets me to Fort Smith. But I offer double bounty, two thousand dollars, to the man that turns me loose!"

Aldridge and Moonlight reined toward the wagon and looked at the prisoner with curious, steel-tipped glints in their eyes.

" You hear me?" the assassin yelled in desperation. " I'm offerin' you two thousand dollars, just for turnin' the key in these chains. I've got the money. In gold. All you have to do is take the key from that cowhand!"

Able Moonlight fastidiously parted his beard and spat into the brush. " Gettin' on toward dark," he observed tone-lessly.

Oren rode up, leading his boss's bay quarter horse. " What's the excitement?" he asked, shooting an interested glance in Bobby Jack's direction.

" No excitement," Aldridge said, taking the lead rope from Oren. " You go with Huck and look for the geldin'."

Oren glanced at the ridge and was on the verge of observing that night was only minutes away, but in the end he merely looked at Huck and shrugged. Without another word of instruction, the two hands put their mounts up the slope and soon dropped from sight on the other side of the ridge.

"You listen to me!" Bobby Jack screamed, the shrillness of hysteria in his voice. "Two thousand dollars! Think about it, cowhands—how long would it take you to make that much money workin' for Aldridge?"

Able Moonlight, with a sigh of weariness, casually kneed over to the wagon and said coldly, quietly, "Keep your mouth shut, killer. Until I'm out of sight of this wagon, out of the sound of your voice, you keep your mouth shut. You hear me?"

The young assassin blinked, startled at the offhand deadliness that crouched behind the sheriff's words. Moonlight wheeled his mount, nodded to Kiowa and Dobie, touched his broad hatbrim to Amilia Rathmore. "Sorry we gave you so much trouble. . . ." Then, as though realizing the inadequacy of his words, he nodded curtly to Aldridge and the two men headed silently toward the dying sun.

Not until they were well out of sight did Bobby Jack Wilkes make a sound. Then it was to collapse on the wagon bed, sobbing bitter tears of hate and frustration.

Amilia Rathmore lifted her hands and studied their trembling bleakly. Then, self-consciously, she hid the accusing hands behind her. "Thank God," she said gravely. "It's over. It was an honest mistake, I suppose, on the part of that rancher, but it could so easily have ended in tragedy. But now it's over," she said again, as if to convince herself.

She turned a shaky smile in Kiowa's direction, waiting for reassurance. But Kiowa could think of nothing to say. He had seen the light of greed in Huck's eyes, and in Oren's.

CHAPTER FOURTEEN

THAT NIGHT they huddled a little closer than usual about the fire, Kiowa, Amilia Rathmore and the hangman.

"I'm obliged for that yarn you spun for that red-necked cowman, Dobie."

The hangman shrugged his hunched shoulders, indicating that it was of no importance.

Kiowa probed quietly, in search of the hangman's motives. "It wasn't no small thing, Dobie. A hothead like Aldridge would of shot you on the spot if he'd caught you lyin' to him. Court officer or no court officer. You mind tellin' me why you took the chance?"

"Chance?" The hangman grinned loosely. "A man takes pride in what he does well, as the sayin' goes. I'm an executioner—a hangman—and a good one. Maybe the best there is, in this country. Have you ever seen a cow branded with an iron too hot, with a hand too heavy, and the mark won't scab over because the burn's too deep? Then the place festers and runs and the first thing you know it's alive with heel-fly grubs, and the cow is down. You ever see a thing like that, friend?"

"Sure. But not often. A hand that can't handle an iron better'n that don't last long in cow country."

"But you have seen it?"

"I told you," Kiowa said impatiently. "But not as a regular thing."

"A sorry job of brandin'. Kind of goes against the grain, don't it?"

"Sure, it would go against the grain." Kiowa scowled.

"There you are," the hangman said. "Your trade's tendin' cattle. Mine's hangin'. I hate a shade-tree lynchin' the way you do a botched brand."

Well, Kiowa thought wryly, every man to his own trade, his own brand of pride. He walked away from the fire, got the horses and staked them closer to the wagon. They were down to two animals now; better to keep them where he could see them. When he got back to the fire, Dobie had already turned in.

"A funny bird," Kiowa said to Amilia Rathmore. "You wouldn't think he had the grit to stand up to a gent like that cowman, would you?"

Miss Rathmore frowned. "You heard what he said. It wasn't courage that prompted his intervention. It was sadism . . . that's all."

Kiowa grunted, shrugged and hunkered down by the fire. "Maybe," he said wearily, scratching his bristling jaw. "But he did stand up to Aldridge, and he did lie about the horses and save my neck. And I won't soon forget that."

Amilia Rathmore ducked her head, embarrassed and ashamed, but she couldn't bring herself to offer a kind word for the hangman. For several minutes they were silent. Kiowa listened to the wind slipping quietly over the dark, wooded hills. It had been a long day, a hard day, and the less he thought about it from here on in, the better he would like it.

"Is it over, Mr. Jones?" Amilia Rathmore asked with her customary bluntness.

Kiowa looked up, blinking. "Over? We're still a good ways from Fort Smith."

"That's not what I mean. Is it over with that cattleman, and the sheriff?"

"Yes." Kiowa nodded. "It's over with them. We won't be seein' them any more."

"And the two hands? The red-headed one, and the little man with the bandy legs?"

Kiowa breathed deeply, then reached for makings to give his hands something to do. So she had noticed the one called Huck and the one called Oren. Kiowa hadn't been the only one to notice the way greed had lit up their faces when talk had turned to that double bounty. He might have known. Amilia Rathmore wouldn't likely miss a thing as obvious as that.

Now she was peering at him through those thick lenses. " You're worried, Mr. Jones?"

" Sure I'm worried," Kiowa said with an edge of irritation in his voice. " I've been worried since the day I blundered into these prisoners, and the hard-luck marshal, and I'll go on bein' worried until I get them off my hands and out of my mind."

But it was a waste of time trying to change the subject. " I was thinking of those two hands," she said. " You're expecting them to return, aren't you?"

Kiowa jabbed his twisted cigarette into his mouth and lit it. Then he sighed. " They'll be back. But not to-night. I've seen their kind before. They'll have to worry on it a spell. Then they'll have to hunt up a likely spot to bushwhack us. And that takes time."

" To-morrow?" she asked. It was just a question, with no particular anxiety behind it.

" Maybe." He nodded. " More'n likely it'll be to-morrow, if they can find the right place. They'll want to get in and get it over with, once they decide."

" What will we do?"

Kiowa bared his teeth in a humourless grin. " I don't know, Miss Rathmore." He got to his feet, touching his battered hatbrim. " I guess I'll turn in. You better do the same."

He turned and walked to the far side of the wagon where he had thrown his roll. Wilkes called out, the cockiness back in his voice. " How about it, cowboy? You want to earn that two thousand dollars for yourself, or do you want that red-headed hand and the little bronc peeler to get it?"

So Kiowa and the assassin had been thinking in the same direction. " You're just chokin' to give away that two thousand dollars that you ain't got, ain't you, Wilkes?"

The assassin laughed. " You've got the gold, Jones, and that's just as good. Maybe better. A lot of money—them two men of Aldridge's won't think twice about shootin' you out of the saddle to get their hands on it."

" And after they get it? What use will you be to them

then? What's to stop them from killin' you, along with the rest of us?"

"Greed," the killer said smugly. "I know their kind. That gold will just whet their appetite for more. And I'll promise it to them. I'll tell them anything they want to hear. . . ." He smiled. "Until I get my hands on a gun."

"You got it worked out pretty good," Kiowa admitted. ". . . But I wonder if you got it worked out how to save your neck when old Rupe Dobie puts you on his hangin' machine?"

A brittle silence fell on the dark slope.

: : : :

Kiowa untied his roll, kicked it open and pulled off his boots. He lay on top of the roll, looking up at the ice-blue sky, feeling the damp chill in the early spring night. Two thousand dollars. How many hands of stud could a man draw with that kind of bank behind him? How many turns of the wheel of fortune? How long could he buck the tiger, drink good whisky, living high and wide? How many dance-hall girls could a man get his arms around at one time? Girls with frizzled hair and glittery eyes and voices brassier than fire horns, but soft and white just the same, and willing. How much hell could a good man raise packing that much yellow gold in his money pouch? How much?

Kiowa Jones grinned to himself ruefully. There were two sides to every coin, two ways of looking at every problem, or opportunity. For every rip-roaring drunk there was a skull-cracking hang-over. For every tussle with some lemon-haired saloon girl there were the weeks of anxiety that followed, and maybe something else besides. For every dollar dropped at some crooked wheel of fortune or faro table went the knowledge that you'd been taken for a fool.

It never failed. Two sides to every coin.

Looking at it that way, it wasn't too hard to put aside Bobby Jack's two-thousand-dollar temptation. Still, and all the same, a little ripple of discomfort went up Kiowa's back as he thought about it. Until right now, this very moment, there hadn't *been* any temptation.

That was something to think about. He had stubbornly resisted Amilia Rathmore's pleading to accept the legal bounty for bringing Wilkes to Fort Smith . . . if he got him there. But for a little while he had considered Bobby Jack's offer of double bounty. Only for a moment—that was true—but considered it all the same. And Kiowa knew that he would never again be quite the man that he had been just a few minutes before. He would never again be quite sure that his hardheaded integrity wasn't a mask strapped over the face of shiftlessness, and maybe even cowardice. Maybe the only reason he wasn't a thief, or a hired killer like Wilkes, was that he simply lacked the guts for it. Maybe it was an easy thing, after all, to play the right-thinking, law-abiding cowhand when you sensed all along that you lacked the grit to be anything bigger.

He sat cross-legged on his roll, fumbled with makings and lit a smoke. There was uneasiness in the night and in his own mind. He sensed that he had changed since tying up with the dead marshal's prisoners, and Amilia Rathmore, and Rupe Dobie. Changed. His problems weren't as simple, his life was no longer carefree and pleasant as it had been before. He had become a man with care and responsibilities, and with troubles that he didn't know how to deal with, or even give a name to.

Kiowa glared with uncertain anger at the reddish glow of the campfire on the far side of the wagon. Sleep would be a while in coming—he might as well get up and see if there was any coffee left over from supper.

He was surprised to see that Amilia Rathmore was still at the fire. She sat hunched on an old oak chest that had been salvaged from the storm, the firelight clashing on her lenses as she stared into the dying flame. She looked up, startled to see him standing there beside her.

"Is anything the matter?"

He shrugged, indicating that nothing was wrong. He shook the coffee pot; it was empty. He made no move to fill it, and neither did she. "I figured you'd be in the wagon," he said in a tone that implied that she was intruding on his privacy, instead of it being the other way around.

"I couldn't sleep," she said wearily. "Apparently you couldn't either."

Kiowa hunkered on the opposite side of the fire and they watched each other for several seconds in silence. "It's been some day," he said at last.

She said nothing.

He built another smoke and hung it in the corner of his mouth without lighting it. "Maybe I was wrong about the two hands. That Aldridge, he's all whalebone and rawhide; maybe the hands went lookin' for that geldin' of his, like he told 'em to."

"But you don't believe it, do you?"

Kiowa sighed. No other answer was necessary. He scowled into the fire—he didn't know how fiercely. After a moment Miss Rathmore got to her feet, and there was a raw edge to her voice when she said, "I'm sorry. I'll go to the wagon now."

Kiowa blinked. "Sorry for what?"

"You make it plain enough, Mr. Jones. You want to be alone."

He snorted impatiently. "Don't be a fool, Miss Rathmore. Sit down."

Strangely, instead of flaring in anger, she allowed herself a small smile. "Sit down," he said again, but this time not so rough. And she reclaimed her seat on the battered chest.

He looked at her in a curious way, studying her face, almost as though he were seeing her for the first time. In time, he guessed, a man would get used to those spectacles. They were just something that a man had to adjust himself to—like a McClellan saddle. Suddenly he blurted, "I been kind of wonderin' . . ."

An eyebrow lifted. "Yes, Mr. Jones?"

"Well, you put yourself to a lot of trouble, gone a far piece out of your way, maybe even lost your job up at that Indian school . . ."

"Are you about to bring up the bounty money again, Mr. Jones?"

He grinned uncertainly. "I guess I was. A while ago I got to thinkin' things that I didn't like——"

Coming uncomfortably close to the target, she said, "That double bounty that Mr. Wilkes keeps waving in everybody's face? Greed is an ugly thing; sometimes I think it must be a disease, more contagious than smallpox. You would have been something more than human, Mr. Jones, if you hadn't come down with at least a light case of it." She smiled. "You're over it now?"

Stunned, he nodded.

"But it still bothers you? You're afraid the temptation will return?"

"I ain't no nickel-plated saint. But I want to get that killer, that Wilkes, to Fort Smith. And that's the truth."

Her smiled widened just a little. "I believe you, Mr. Jones."

"I want you to have the bounty," he said abruptly, after a short pause.

She shook her head. "No. I can always get a job teaching school. But that money could set you up in a cattle business, something you know, and take pride in, and are good at." But she saw the wall of stubbornness building up around him and softened her argument. "All right," she relented. "We'll divide it between us. Will that satisfy you?'

"That satisfies me fine." He grinned, then lit the limp cigarette that still dangled from the corner of his mouth. "You've got a level head on you, Miss Rathmore . . . for a woman." He stretched, yawned and scratched himself as the weight of a bad day bore down on him. "Well, I guess I'll hit the feathers. . . ."

Amilia Rathmore, with that curious smile at the corners of her mouth, watched him disappear into the darkness on the other side of the wagon. She had his respect. That was something. A small victory in her continuing war against the bachelorhood of Kiowa Jones. But a victory all the same. And, as Bobby Jack Wilkes was so fond of saying, it was still a long way to Fort Smith.

CHAPTER FIFTEEN

THE WAGON was about a quarter of a mile away, coming slowly toward them, bulling its way through the scrub timber. They couldn't hear it yet. The dry axle had been greased—Kiowa Jones had attended to that. But they could see the veil of dust that rose like thin, hardwood smoke over the brush, and they knew that the wagon was coming.

Oren breathed deeply, with satisfaction. Huck laughed softly. In a matter of minutes the gold would be theirs. They would be rich.

"Two thousand gold," the red-headed cowhand said softly. "Think about that, Oren!"

Oren had been thinking about it. A thousand for himself, a thousand for Huck. Oren looked steadily at his partner's back and thoughtfully stroked the trigger of his saddle gun. A man could do a lot with a thousand dollars. He could do more with two thousand. Oren hadn't quite made up his mind what he was going to do about it.

The two hands had reined up on a brushy slope overlooking a lightly wooded pass between two hills. An old game track, maybe, or an Indian trail.

"Let's move," Huck said. Oren grunted. They put their horses down the rugged incline. Oren reined up behind a sandstone outcropping and drew his saddle gun. Huck rode on down to the bottom of the draw and up the other slope. He too drew his saddle gun, tied his horse out of sight in a brush thicket and then, on foot, made his way back along the slope until he was directly opposite his partner. Oren took off his hat and waved it. Huck waved his carbine to show that he understood. The wagon was nearing the pass.

They had talked it over between them, planned the dry-gulching to the point where mistakes were no longer a factor. First they would drop the team. Then the cowhand, Jones. Finally the schoolteacher, the hangman and the prisoners, taking them as they came, making certain that no one was left alive to carry the story to a federal judge.

There had been some difference of opinion about what to do with Bobby Jack Wilkes. Oren had been for letting the assassin live, at least for a little while, on the chance of getting something added to that double bounty. Huck had been for killing Wilkes on the spot, with the others. Play it safe. Take the gold and then set out after that grey gelding of Aldridge's, as if nothing had happened. It sounded so simple and foolproof that, in the end, Oren had agreed to string along with his partner. In a few days they'd find the gelding and head back for the Aldridge headquarters, two conscientious, hard-working cowboys looking after their boss's property. Who was to suspect them of murder and robbery?

Oren, still in the saddle, peered over the top of the outcropping and saw the wagon enter the confining V of the gun-sight pass. He grinned to himself, levering a cartridge into the chamber of his carbine. Jones and the schoolteacher were on the spring seat. The storm-tattered wagon sheet flapped limply over the bows. Dobie and the prisoners would be riding inside, under the sheet, but that didn't matter. With Jones and the schoolteacher out of the way, the others could be killed at will.

The schoolteacher's face was hidden beneath the hood of her sunbonnet. Jones slouched gracelessly against a wagon bow, his wide-brim hat pulled low on his forehead. He looked all in. Oren laughed soundlessly. You're about to get a rest, Jones. A long, long rest. . . . He sighted carefully along the barrel of his saddle gun.

Over on the far slope Huck was also observing Jones's attitude of exhaustion with grim amusement. First the team, then Jones, then the schoolteacher. . . . The distance was too great to make out the expressions on their faces. That was too bad. It would have been interesting to see how the cowhand took it, when the bullets began to fly.

Huck sat on the ground at the edge of a jack oak thicket. The air was still. No windage was necessary as he adjusted his sights. A perfect day for shooting. A vagrant thought crossed the red-headed cowhand's mind, and he grinned widely to himself. How many times had Bobby Jack Wilkes waited out situations just like this one, watching some unsuspecting victim over his sights, his finger on the trigger?

It was almost time. Huck glanced at his partner on the far slope. Oren tended to be the least bit reckless at times. And greedy. A good partner in a lot of ways, and they'd worked together off and on for years, but just the same, greed and recklessness could be dangerous things. It had also crossed Huck's mind that a man with two thousand dollars in his pocket was considerably richer than a man with only one thousand.

Oren waved his hat again. The wagon was directly below. Huck pumped his rifle over his head, then settled over the sights and squeezed the trigger.

The roar of the saddle gun was surprisingly loud. Huck was pleased to see the near horse drop in the traces without a kick. Oren, from behind the outcropping, fired almost at the same instant. The second half of Amilia Rathmore's prized wagon team went down.

Huck, with the roar of excitement in his ears, quickly levered another cartridge and fired again. He saw the cowhand twist awkwardly on the wagon seat and slump to the floor boards. That took care of Jones.

Amilia Rathmore, apparently frozen with fear, sat motionless while Oren drew a bead and fired his second round. The impact of the bullet knocked her off the seat and she fell to the floor boards with Jones. Neither of them moved.

Huck jumped to his feet and waved excitedly to Oren, and Oren waved back, grinning. Everything had gone perfectly. They couldn't have wished for better. They took aim again and emptied their magazines into the covered part of the wagon. Nothing moved. Horses, wagon, passengers—a dead stillness lay over everything. Huck and Oren reloaded their saddle guns, then Huck hurried back to the thicket where he had left his horse. Perfect. Everything had gone off without the smallest hitch.

The two men mounted and descended cautiously to the V of the pass, carbines at the ready, just in case someone might still be alive in the back of the wagon.

"What do you think?" Huck asked, eyeing the wagon.

Oren grinned. "I got to hand it to you. They come through this pass, just like you said. I got to hand it to you for that."

Huck would have felt easier if Oren had found something to complain about. Backslapping wasn't Oren's way, unless maybe he had a knife in his hand.

"Better have a look in the back of the wagon."

"Then we look for the gold."

That greed again. A dangerous thing. Yes, sir, Huck thought to himself, when this thing's over I might have to make some plans for Oren. But not just now. Not until the money was in their hands and this business of murder was behind them.

Frowning, Oren reined up a short distance from the wagon.

"What is it?" Huck asked.

Oren grunted, tightening his grip on the carbine. "Somethin's gone sour. I can feel it."

"What could go sour? Everything worked out just the way I told you."

"Just the way you told me," Oren repeated, with a note of sarcasm. "I can feel a thing when it's bad—and I feel it now."

"You're loco," Huck told him, but not with the cocksure tone that he had used before. It was true that Oren had an instinct for hard-luck situations. Bed-grounds where cattle would spook and run for no reason at all. Innocent-looking little creeks with quicksand traps that could swallow a team and wagon in a matter of minutes. He had a knack for smelling out such things.

"Let's get down and have a look under that wagon sheet."

They stepped down to the ground. The horses, smelling blood, shied nervously, and Huck tied them in the brush while Oren, growing tense, covered the area with his rifle. "All right," Huck said, "throw back the wagon sheet. I'll cover you."

Oren stepped to the rear of the wagon, coldly fired five times through the puckered opening, then jerked the tattered canvas to one side. There was a long, tense moment of silence as Oren stared into the wagon box, saying nothing.

"What is it?" Huck asked impatiently.

Oren broke into a fit of savage cursing, ran to the front of the wagon and climbed over the wheel, peering down at the motionless figures on the floor boards. At last he turned to his partner and snarled, "Dummies!"

Huck blinked. Then the ugly truth bored into his mind. He flung back the canvas and looked inside the wagon. Empty! With mounting wildness, he darted to the front of the wagon and climbed the wheel opposite Oren.

Now they knew why Jones had looked so limp and exhausted, why Amilia Rathmore's face had been so completely hidden beneath the hood of her bonnet. They had been dummies, made from odds and ends of bedding and clothing.

Hate in Oren's eyes stabbed like knives. "So you planned it so there couldn't be any mistakes, did you!"

Huck's face was curiously pale. He looked sick. He worked his mouth, tried to speak, but before he could make a sound his partner had shot him twice, once in the stomach and once in the chest. With a groan, Huck dropped his saddle gun. His numb hands released their hold on the wagon box and he fell over the wheel to the ground.

Kiowa Jones, rising up in a brush-covered draw on the near slope, put his rifle to his shoulder and said, "Hold steady, Oren. Don't make me kill you."

After a moment of electric anger, Oren very carefully placed his saddle gun on the wagon seat and climbed down. "It was a trick!" he said hoarsely, accusing his dead partner. "A dirty, rotten Apache trick, makin' dummies, startin' the team through the draw, then layin' out to get the drop on us!" He wheeled angrily on Kiowa. "You knowed all the time we'd be layin' for you here, didn't you?"

Kiowa shrugged wearily. "This draw was in our line of march and tailor-made for dry-gulchin'. I figured you and your partner would find it." He looked sadly at the horses lying dead in the harness. "Killin' the team was somethin' I didn't figure on. I don't guess you and your partner'll mind if we use your horses the rest of the way to Fort Smith, will you?" He gestured for Oren to drop his revolver.

Oren, his monkey face glistening, unbuckled his cartridge belt and let it fall. "You're callin' the tune, for now. Where's the others at?"

"On the back trail, maybe half a mile." Kiowa raised his rifle and fired three evenly spaced rounds at the sky. "That ought to bring 'em in."

Oren looked around at the surrounding slopes, then sneered at Kiowa. "A goddamn hero," he said bitterly. "Layin' out there in a gully all this time, waitin' for me and Huck to make our play. A run-down-at-the-heels grubline rider. Where'd you ever get the notion you was a hero, Jones?"

Kiowa bared his teeth in an angry grin. "It was easy—you and your partner playin' right into my hands. Too bad, Oren. You ought to of stuck to cattle."

Oren laughed abruptly, a sound as hard as hailstones. "You'll never get me to Arkansas, Jones, if that's what you've got in mind."

"I'm beginnin' to get a little bit tired," Kiowa said softly, "of people tellin' me what I can't do."

After a few minutes the bedraggled figure of Amilia Rathmore appeared at the far end of the draw. "Mr. Jones!" She came toward them, her sunbonnet fluttering in the breeze like some drab battle pennant. "Mr. Jones!" She threw herself at the startled Kiowa and nearly bowled him over. She had a strangle hold on his neck, clinging to him with the hysteria of a drowning person going down for the third time. Her eyes were wet, and this seemed to disturb her more than anything else. "I was afraid . . . When we heard the shooting, I thought . . ."

"I'm all right, Miss Rathmore," Kiowa said uncomfortably. "It's all over. They didn't touch me."

She looked at him blearily. "You aren't wounded? You're sure?"

"I'm sure," he said, wondering how he was going to get himself untangled. Worrying about how this kind of thing might look to others. "Where's Dobie? You leave him back with the prisoners?"

She looked blank, then nodded. "Yes. Back with the prisoners." She looked at him, smiling weakly, and Kiowa sighed relief. Maybe now he could get out of this tangle of female arms. But just as she seemed to take hold of herself, she burst into tears.

Kiowa muttered to himself about the perverseness of women. "Now look here, Miss Rathmore . . ." Awkwardly, he put his arms around her and tried to think of something to say. But by the time he got the words straight in his mind he had discovered that it wasn't so tough after all, having a woman in his arms.

: : : :

They slanted north-east through the Choctaw Nation, putting the railroad and its thin veneer of civilization behind them, riding the high line, dodging the travelled roads, as wary of strangers as a highwayman one jump ahead of a posse. Huck's and Oren's saddle horses were in harness now, dragging the dilapidated wagon through the brush, from ridge to ridge.

Kiowa, riding up front with Miss Rathmore, peered under the wagon sheet from time to time to see how Dobie and the prisoners were doing. The hangman's professional interest had shifted, at least temporarily, from Wilkes to Oren.

"Killin' your partner that way, in front of a witness. A capital crime, friend. That's how the old judge'll read it, when we get you to Fort Smith."

Oren snarled, lunging in his chains. "Get your bill out of me, you buzzard!"

Bobby Jack Wilkes laughed mirthlessly. He hated Dobie's guts. Just the same, it was a pleasure to watch him working on somebody else for a change.

As the road to Arkansas became shorter, Levi Skoda became less concerned with the mysteries of tarot. For hours at a time he would lie back in the wagon box, his eyes closed, listening to Amabel's muted laughter. Ghosts of Amabel worked like silvery worms in his brain. He no longer thought of anything else. He only wished for the trip to end, for the hangman to take him. He wanted rest, and quiet, peace. He began to look upon Rupe Dobie as a friend.

Kiowa Jones had thoughts of his own, disturbing thoughts, as he held a steady north-east course. He caught himself sneaking quick glances at Amilia Rathmore from beneath the pulled-down brim of his hat. Stubbornly, he fixed his gaze on the plodding team and didn't as much as grunt for several minutes.

". . . Is something the matter, Mr. Jones?"

Something was sure as live-fire hell the matter, all right, but he didn't know what. Leastwise, he didn't understand it. "I been thinkin'," he muttered at last, more to himself than to her.

She removed her spectacles and peered nearsightedly at his craggy face. "What about, Mr. Jones?"

He held the lines between his knees and built himself a crooked smoke. "Just thinkin'. That's all. About the last time I was in Tascosa, the time I had. About the time I rode bogs all spring with a greener from Kansas that was tryin' to learn to play the jews'-harp. About some good horses I've knowed, and men too. About how good coffee tastes early in the mornin' before you start out to ride circle. Things like that."

He found a match in his hatband and lit his smoke.

She said cautiously, "The way you've lived and worked, the things you've done, they're important to you, aren't they?"

Kiowa shot her a guarded look. "It's all I know."

Suddenly she looked away. "It won't be long before we reach Arkansas," she said stiffly. "Then you can go back to being a cowhand."

"That's just the trouble," he said gruffly, staring straight ahead. "I don't want to go back to tendin' the other fellow's cows. And I'm tired sleepin' on the ground half the time, usin' my back for a mattress and my belly for a blanket. And I'm sick of line-camp cookin', and buckshot beans, and dry-salt pork that gets so strong it could throw and tie a yearlin' bull."

". . . I see," she said, in a surprisingly small voice.

He turned and glared at her. "Look," he demanded, "you got it in your mind to head someplace special when we get to Fort Smith? *If* we get there? Someplace, I mean, besides that Indian school at Tahlequah?"

She swallowed with difficulty, shaking her head.

"Well, here's the way I see it," Kiowa said loudly, as though he were daring her to oppose him. "Seems like we hit it off pretty good, everything considered. What's to stop us from poolin' our bounty money when we get it and leasin' a piece of range from the Cherokees? I know some Kansas cowmen that might stake me to a good bull and maybe fifteen, twenty head of she stuff." Sensing that this was a delicate subject, Kiowa quickly tried to smooth it over. "I mean, that's how cows are. You throw 'em in with the bull and the next spring you go out and count the increase."

"I understand," Amilia Rathmore said in a curiously pitched voice.

Kiowa looked relieved. He stared at her for several seconds, then finally said, "Well, what about it?"

"Mr. Jones," she asked quietly, "is this a proposal of marriage?"

He glared at her. "Of course it is. What did you think it was?"

She shook her head dumbly.

"I guess it surprises you," he said, scratching his tender neck. "I'll tell you somethin' else—it surprises me too. I guess I just got fed up with things, the way they was goin'. Don't ask me when I decided. I don't know."

But he knew. When she had hung on to his neck, looking at him like he was somebody, not just a saddle bum. That was when he knew that he'd had enough of things as they'd been going. "What about it, Miss Rathmore? Is it a deal?"

"My name's Amilia." She nodded solemnly. "Yes, it's a deal."

He grinned self-consciously and put his arm about her waist. Suddenly he dropped the lines to the floor of the wagon and let them lie. "I reckon," he said, "the horses can blunder along by theirselves for a while."

THE END